Dreamhaven

By

Tracy Tandy

Illustrations By Cara Bevan

Inevitable Ink Publishing

San Rafael, California

Dreamhaven

Published in the United States by Inevitable Ink Publishing

San Rafael, California.

www.inevitableinkpublishing.com

Library of Congress Catalog Control Number: 2015904962
Metadata: fantasy; dreams—fiction; cats—fiction;
transformation—fiction; young artists—fiction
Paperback ISBN: 978-0-9961758-0-7
Ebook ISBN: 978-0-9961758-1-4

Illustrations by Cara Bevan
Cover Design by Cara Bevan & Daniel Cook Design
Interior Design by Lucy Arnold
Author Photo by Mark Morris

For Peach

Who taught me that love
has the best imagination of all.

Acknowledgements

The road to Dreamhaven is paved with kindness. Many people generously contributed their time and insights to turn tattered pages and red ink into a real story. There is no more fertile ground than weekly time with Christine Harvey, Cary Sparks and Wendy Young-Howard. Tammy Kaehler also provided key edits undiluted by distance. My thanks to each of you for years of support, your perceptive critiques and your inspiring prose. I'm honored to write beside you and I can't wait to read your next books.

Cara Bevan, *Illustrator Extraordinaire*, is an author's miracle. Her brilliant imagination and meticulous artistry have brought the denizens of Dreamhaven to life—fur, fang and all. And who knew you'd be the one to catch all those typos?

I owe very special thanks to Lucy Arnold, who encouraged me to "pick up the pen," has held my hand ever since, and most recently came to my rescue with her remarkable artist's eye to design and implement every page.

Melissa and Joycelyn, thanks for holding me close. And Leslie Keenan for asking, "Is there a Book in You?" Turned out there are many. Essential readers along the way include Mary Elmstrom, Rosemary Hart, Gerry Okimoto, Veronica Smith, Holly Stanaland, Laurie Tandy and her inspiring students. Julie Arnold, thank you for your beautiful web design. Daniel Cook, thank you for your expertise and gorgeous cover work.

Thank you, my characters, each and every one, for coming to me on the page and in my dreams to whisper your story in my ear. Thank you teachers, librarians, booksellers and readers everywhere. Dreamhaven would exist only in my heart without you.

And yes, Mark is shamelessly named after my husband—because he is my constant and everlasting hero.

Table of Contents

CHAPTER ONE

Out Cat

Nick startled awake and rolled to his paws beneath the hedge. He might not have nine lives like every other cat, but he could count. And right now he counted three angry Siamese—one male, two females. Nick had spent the day watching the pampered purebreds doze in their garden, bellies up, basking in the spring sunshine. They'd had no idea an eight-pound Russian Blue spied on them.

Or that Nick envied every moment they slept, effortlessly traveling through their dreams to reach their other eight lives. Nick didn't travel when he slept. He was trapped in this one life.

And his disability made him notorious in catdom, a target for bullies of all breeds.

He must have dozed off and cried out in his sleep, because now the three Siamese crouched just feet away, all big fur and no-nonsense snarls. Nick sighed. They might have a few lives to spare, but he had just this one. At a year old, Nick was fast, and sizing up challengers was a skill he'd learned early and used often. He charged the male and locked him down before the other two cats could move.

The Siamese salvaged their pride with dramatic hisses and impressive teeth, but Nick knew they were all mouth and no bite. He backed away to begin his journey home.

Outside the garden, Nick waited in the shadows for two women in long hoopskirts to pass, and then dodged a horse cart to cross the cobbled road. He stepped through a wrought iron gate and leapt to a wooden fence rail to begin his trek across London. He thought about the Siamese cats' day: thirteen stalked birds, five now-tailless lizards, constant grooming, four naps apiece—and how many adventures in their other lives? Nick could only imagine.

"I'm getting nowhere!" he growled.

He wanted to please his dad. Nick owed him that. But after endless hours secretly studying other cats, he still hadn't discovered anything they had that he didn't. Every other feline just fell asleep, stepped through dream and woke up in one of their nine lives. Simple. That's the way it had worked since the world began.

Except for Nick.

And he was no closer to understanding why.

"Hisssssss!"

Nick looked left, straight into the eyes of a young Abyssinian challenging him from a brick window ledge.

"I'm just headed home, don't want any trouble," Nick made his tone easy and kept walking.

"You're broken and hideously ugly, you are, and—"

The Abyssinian obviously looked forward to a lengthy exchange of pre-fight slurs and spitting. Nick usually turned a deaf ear to punks this young, but tonight he was low on patience. Before the cat could drum up his next insult, Nick unsheathed his claws, shifted his weight and leaped to the window ledge.

The shocked Abyssinian recoiled, his claws catching in the frothy white curtains. He teetered for a moment and then fell backward through the open window, ripping a long tear in the sheer fabric on his way to the kitchen floor.

Nick indulged in a small smile at the sound of claws scrabbling on polished wood. But his good humor faded away as fast as it had come.

He was so sick of his one pathetic life.

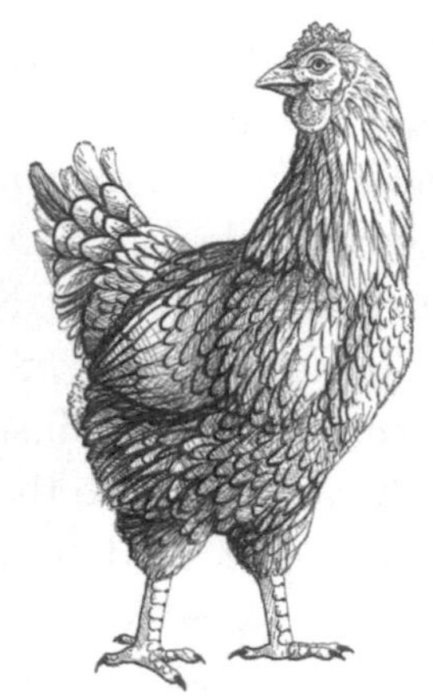

Not So
Home Sweet...

Nick reached the Tower of London grounds and climbed the White Tower from one step stone to the next. Two-dozen feet above the ground, he arrived at a crown-shaped hole cut into the thick stones of the wall. He paused to look out over the river and the darkening sky, watching gas lamps flutter to life in a scattered pattern, as lamplighters moved across the city. Hunger urged him inside, but Nick was reluctant to give up the easy peace of the outdoors. He stepped through the hole and into a complex stone labyrinth. Five minutes later he emerged in the Tower kitchen.

"…but no such luck. He's back," his mother smirked.

"Home sweet home," Nick said under his breath.

His mother, Mona, was a compact calico in a perpetual snit. Thanks to Nick's disability, the cat community constantly talked about her, but not in a nice way. Mona was furious with Nick for being born different, and she never missed an opportunity to rebuke him.

"If I'd had other kittens, they'd have been perfect and respectable," she liked to remind Nick—and every cat within earshot.

When he was a kitten, Mona cuffed and nipped him out of spite. Nick had run away more than once, but his father had always found him and coaxed him home. By now, Mona knew better than to attack Nick, but she took her anger out on his dad instead.

Nick waited, and Mona didn't disappoint.

"There are no Russian Blues in my bloodline," she spat as blue-eyed Nick, fur tinged blue from tip to tail, walked past her in the kitchen. Mona was convinced that Nick's rare coloring was a choice he'd made just to further embarrass her. "He is *your* fault," she again notified her long-suffering mate.

Nick's dad, Byron, was a magnificent grey and black tabby, a big animal, and all muscle. Ignoring his sneering wife, he nodded his son over to join him at the bronze food bowl, a gift from their mistress, Queen Victoria.

"How did it go today?" Byron asked.

Nick crossed the huge kitchen to crouch beside his father. "Hmmm, fine. Nothing new." Nick kept his tone nonchalant, and his head down, eyes firmly fixed on his food.

Father and son continued to chew in amiable silence, but when Nick looked up from his meal, Byron sat staring at him.

The big cat seemed to come to a decision, but he only smiled and licked Nick between the ears. Then, as he always did at twilight, he curled up on the feather bed behind the stove to enjoy a catnap before work.

Byron worked for the British Government, and his official title was "Guardian of the Tower Ravens." In Great Britan, the Tower Ravens were legendary, and so was Nick's dad. Some believed the Ravens had magic powers to preserve the British Empire, and to ensure they remained at the Tower, their black wings were clipped. The Ravens were carefully protected and fully aware of their status.

Over the centuries, many animals had been assigned to eliminate predators and trespassers breaching the Ravens' rookery on the Tower roof. But the birds had driven off every proposed nighttime guardian, with the unlikely exception of one species: Cat.

In the six years Byron had held his post, the Ravens' enemies had learned to fear him, and the royal children had demanded the right to feed him.

When he awoke, Byron called to Nick in his firm voice. "Nick, if you're willing, I'd like you to join me on the roof tonight," he said.

Nick had been washing his left ear, but stopped mid-stroke. He wasn't sure he'd heard right. He turned to look into his father's striped face.

"Me? Go to the roof with you?" Byron nodded once. Nick shot to his feet.

"Good. I'll explain on the way," laughed Byron.

Shoulder to shoulder, father and son left the kitchen, ignoring Mona's disapproving headshake.

Nick had never officially been allowed in other parts of the

Tower, but he'd snuck behind his father a few times, until he'd been caught and sent back to the kitchen. But now, as he observed his father's awareness of every sight and sound, Nick finally understood that his father had known all along, and allowed Nick to track his footsteps across the worn stones to the first landing.

"I've been thinking about your situation, Nick. I thought if you watched other cats, you could learn to travel in your dreams and reach your other lives. But that doesn't seem to be working, does it?"

Nick nodded once, dropped his eyes to hide his shame, and tightened his lips to keep from blurting out his secret: not only had Nick never reached his other lives in dream, but each time he fell asleep, he had the same horrific nightmare. A shiver ran down Nick's back at the thought of his nightmare, and he faltered in his tracks. He had to run to catch up with his dad.

"I've also noticed that your naps are shorter than the rest of ours, yet you have more energy than any cat I've ever met."

Nick's head snapped up. "I do?"

"Yes, you do. That's one of the reasons I think you might make a very fine Guardian."

When his father's words reached his brain, Nick came to a stunned stop. He couldn't believe what he'd heard.

"We have to keep walking, Nick, it's a long way to the roof, and we can't be late."

Nick put his paws in motion again. A Guardian! His father thought he could be a Guardian. Nick felt lighter than he had in very long time. He felt as if he could skip walking and fly to the roof instead.

"When you were still very young, it occurred to me that your short naps could be a useful advantage. You'd be able to stay vigilant for long hours."

Nick stopped again. "When I was very young? Why didn't you say something then?"

Byron kept walking, and answered when Nick caught up beside him.

"Because the job requires other well-developed skills: courage, good judgment, fighting experience and speed. Now we know that you have plenty of each, or you wouldn't have survived your first year."

They were crossing a landing Nick had never reached before. He looked down over the edge of the steps. The entry hall was just a soft blur of candlelight below him. They started up another staircase.

"I've always hoped I would pass the job to my son, but—and you must truly understand this—it's not my decision."

"So who—?"

"The Ravens, Nick. It's their decision. Always has been."

"A *bird* gets to decide who gets your job?"

"Once you spend some time with them, you'll soon discover that the Tower Ravens are not like any birds you've ever met. Their kind has lived on earth a very long time, watching the world change. They're intelligent, and they pass down their wisdom to every new generation. They're more than birds, really."

"If they're not birds, what are they?"

"I guess I can't explain now. But you'll know what I mean before you leave the roof tonight."

Nick's opinion of birds didn't include intelligence. And wisdom was out of the question. Most of the birds he'd met had ended up as his supper.

Byron came to a halt, smiling as if he could read Nick's thoughts. They'd reached the last landing, and only a single flight of stairs rose into the darkness ahead of them.

"I promise, you'll understand before the night is done, son. They've agreed to meet you, and that alone is a very hopeful sign." Byron brought his nose close to Nick's. He spoke in a hushed, solemn voice.

"You must show the Ravens deep respect, Nick. You must speak only if you are spoken to. And you must remain perfectly still no matter how close they come to you. Once we reach the roof, they will be in control, and I will not be able to help you."

The intensity of his father's gaze scared Nick almost as much as his words. He felt the fur along his neck and tail begin to rise.

His father's voice was gentle when he spoke again.

"If you'd rather not continue, you can stop right here, and follow our trail back home. If that's your decision, I won't ever mention this night again—to anyone. And I will still love you, son."

Nick took a deep breath, and closed his eyes. He didn't want to turn around and go back down the staircases. He wanted to run like his tail was on fire and not stop until he reached the stove and had his back pushed safely up against the stone wall. Birds or no birds, Nick had seen enough of the Tower Ravens to know their shiny beaks were fast and lethal.

But this was his father asking him to be brave. After all the pain he'd caused, he had a chance to make his father proud of him. And if he were the Ravens' Guardian, the other cats would have to accept—no, respect him. His father must have thought of that too. That must be why he'd asked the Ravens to meet Nick.

Nick's spine tingled with fear right down into his paws. Before he could change his mind, he opened his eyes.

"I'll do it."

His father smiled and licked the spot between Nick's ears.

"Then let's go. And no matter what happens, son, I'm proud of you."

Nick stepped onto the final stairway awash in the glow of his father's praise.

If the ol' birds were so smart, maybe they'd know how he could get past his nightmare to live his other lives.

Mark

Seven hundred miles away as a raven flies, Mark Farrallon awoke in Dreamhaven. Spectacular dreams were one thing nine-year-old Mark could count on. And whether his dreams sent him diving for treasure in uncharted seas, or racing across desert sands atop a camel, Mark could also count on finding his best friend, Shift, grinning beside him.

Mark was tall and strong for his age, and his detailed drawings often surprised people. Shift was a shy animal, ten inches high and armored all the way from his chest to the tip of his foot-long tail. Shift liked to change his head and upper body at least once a dream. One night he'd show up with the bandit face and handy paws of a raccoon. The next he'd be a smiling lynx. Mark never knew what face his friend would wear, but he didn't care, because Shift was always smart, brave and loyal.

Mark began each morning the same way: he'd wake up, grab his notebook and pencils, and begin to draw the vivid scenes of their latest dream. Once he'd sketched enough to remember the basics, he'd get dressed and race down the narrow wooden steps from his sleeping loft to the kitchen of his family's cottage. Seated on a bench at the kitchen table, his brown eyes squeezed tight to capture every detail, he would tell his mother, Minette, his latest adventure. Minette cooked breakfast, and asked a question here and there, her blue eyes soft with contentment.

Mark's father, Sean, was a practical man and the village forester. In the spring, fall and summer, he would rise from the table before Mark had finished breakfast, kiss his wife and son and leave their cottage to work in the woods until dark. Only the bitterest cold of winter kept his father from the forest.

Sean had a different name for his son's stories and pictures, "over-imagination." Mark enjoyed every minute with Shift in their dreams together, but Sean had become increasingly frustrated with them. Minette had negotiated an agreement between father and son: as long as Mark did his schoolwork and chores, his father wouldn't complain about time spent writing and drawing. The truce was working, but Mark still felt the tension between them, and he often took refuge in his loft bedroom.

Mark would light his lantern to read the stories of Sir Walter Scott, or Mr. Dickens. Sometimes he'd draw his own illustrations for classics like Ivanhoe or Robinhood—with Shift and he as the heroes. And all on their own they'd discovered strange huts in the woods and floating ships made of exotic debris. They often came upon hidden caves that led deep into the Earth where they visited secret tribes and explored underground cities stretching for miles...

From his loft window, Mark could usually see a scattering of candlelit cottages down the hill in Dreamhaven. And atop the hillside across the river, the red oil light of Clavier's Beacon glowed bright. Mark could picture the statue of Clavier and the ruby light in her outstretched hand. Her beacon had been a guide for mountain travelers for centuries, and the difference between life and death for many.

In a village famous for dreams, Mark and Shift had no doubt theirs were outstanding. Even when a dream took place in the familiar lanes of Dreamhaven, just being with Shift was sure to scare up some fun. Closing his eyes to sleep was Mark's favorite part of every day. Each night, he'd fall into dream and find himself at the foot of a pine tree exactly like the real one beside the cottage. And Shift was always there, waiting for him. Mark knew Shift only existed in his dreams, and that had never been a problem for either of them.

CHAPTER FOUR

Gone Dreamin'

Mark collapsed atop the bed in his starlit room, letting himself drift into the comfort of sleep. Shift met him in the usual place beside the pine tree, and tonight he was wearing the upper body of a red fox. They fell into step as if they'd never been parted and Mark's waking life didn't exist. The crescent moon and unusual star patterns overhead were perfect for a night of summer fun.

"What ya wanna do tonight?" Mark asked.

"Well…" Shift began as he settled into Mark's pace, "we could row down the river in the moonlight."

"Or visit Clavier's Beacon," Mark added.

"Or we could leave a false trail for Dempsey," Shift offered in an innocent voice. Mark snorted, and Shift broke into a wicked, vulpine grin, thinking of the bloodhound tromping through the woods all night.

"Shift," Mark said in his best imitation of a lecturing adult, shaking a finger at his best friend, "you know, that's just too mean to poor ol' Dempsey." He dropped his finger and his tone. "Besides, we did it last week."

They'd been walking aimlessly, but Mark stopped, raising his head to look up. Shift's luminous gaze followed. The night sky blazed with millions of stars. But astronomers on Earth had never seen any of them.

"Or we could—" Mark began.

"—make some new constellations," Shift finished.

Mark lay down on his back, one hand tucked behind his head. Shift rested his head on Mark's other shoulder with a happy grin.

"So what'll it be this time?" Mark asked.

"I think what this galaxy needs is more seafood. At the very least, one giant squidapus," Shift answered with enthusiasm.

"And a long-tailed, fire-breathing, saber-toothed sea dragon—right about…there," Mark pointed.

Shift traced Mark's index finger to the spot in the sky where stars were already in motion. A hooded green eye appeared, blinking down at them. Mark smiled when Shift's scaled tail rattled in approval. Then they got down to some serious star shifting.

Much later, Mark reached out to stroke Shift's soft face. But his fingers found only his own jacket. Shift was gone.

Mark groaned. He knew his cottage bedroom glowed with dawn, but he refused to open his eyes. He pulled the thick comforter over his head to hold on to the last remnants of his dream.

CHAPTER FIVE

The Ravens

All his life, Nick had heard his father talk about the Ravens, and at a safe distance, the birds had seemed only arrogant and unfriendly. But from their perch on the wall six feet above him, their coal black eyes staring straight into Nick's, the Tower Ravens were a nightmare of deadly beaks and sharp claws. Nick tried not to tremble as his father presented him. A year spent defending himself against one or more attackers had taught Nick self-control, and only that discipline allowed him to tear his eyes from the Ravens long enough to bow his head in formal greeting.

Nick heard his father's familiar rumble in his ear, but he'd never before imagined uncertainty in that voice. Nick grew more nervous.

"Nick, please sit down where you are, and remain perfectly still. If you do that, you'll be safe."

Nick wanted to turn and look into his father's eyes, but he knew from the knot in his belly, that his test had already begun. As if on a signal, all seven Ravens spread their wings until they touched wingtip to wingtip, and Nick understood: there would be no escape until the Ravens released him.

Then Nick saw black beaks swooping at his face. He slammed his eyes shut and closed his throat down tight, stifling his cry of terror. He tensed for the pain. But none came.

Nick opened his eyes to find three silent Ravens standing a foot in front of him. Each bird gazed at him with unreadable black eyes. He could feel the other four Ravens at his back. Nick forced himself to picture them just staring, because that was better than all the alternatives he could imagine. Up close, the smallest birds came to Nick's chin, and the largest Raven, who stood directly in front of Nick, looked down his beak into Nick's eyes.

"This isn't so bad," he convinced himself. "If they stay back and keep those beaks to themselves…"

"Rawk rawk, rawk rawk rawwww."

Nick couldn't guess what triggered the first Raven call. The harsh chorus sounded like a war cry exploding in the night, and each one rattled him to his bones, terrifying him. For a very long time, Nick's world narrowed to intermittent piercing Raven voices and the click of talons on stone.

Once, the circle of Ravens shifted and tightened until the four who had been behind Nick now stood inches from his face. The Ravens' eyes never left his, and Nick knew that if he moved, sharp talons would respond with blinding speed. Nick grew thirsty and, despite his fear, he felt drained. But, as the stars wheeled overhead, he did not move.

At some invisible signal, six Ravens resumed their perch on the wall in a rush of wings and hoarse rasps. Nick felt relieved to have the black circle broken. Then his terror moved up a notch.

The lead Raven again stood in front of Nick. The bird leaned forward until his beady eyes and curved beak were a fur's breadth from Nick's nose. The dusty smell of bird was overpowering. Nick felt his claws start to extend against his will. Just when he felt he had to lash out, or suffocate in the bird's dark scent, the Raven opened his wings and rose straight up off the stone floor, hovering a long moment, before taking his place in the center of the others on the wall.

Byron was suddenly beside Nick. "You can stretch now if you'd like, son," he whispered.

Instead Nick turned his head to look a question into his father's eyes.

"You were very brave, Nick. I couldn't be more proud of you."

"So I passed the test? Does that mean we can go now? I'm really hungry."

"We're almost done. First we need to hear the Ravens' verdict, and then you can go. I have to remain at my post for another hour, until dawn."

Nick's jaw dropped. "Dawn?" he whispered. "No wonder I'm so—"

A rustle of wings snapped Nick to attention.

The lead Raven looked into Byron's eyes, ignoring Nick as if he didn't exist. Then the old bird spoke in a voice that sounded like metal on stone. "He is brave, and a credit to you, Guardian Byron."

Nick's body tingled with pride. Byron took a deep breath, his already generous ruff swelling at the Raven leader's words.

"But he will never be Our guardian."

Beside him, Nick felt his father sway.

"What? What does he mean?" Nick asked his father in a voice that echoed off the stones. "You said I was brave. That means I passed, right?"

A ripple moved through the black wings above the two cats, and seven beaks opened, poised.

"Nick, we'll talk as soon as I get home. This is not the—"

"NO! I did my best. But it's still not enough. It'll never be enough." Nick turned and raced to the entry hole. Blind with shame and rage he threw himself down the stone stairs at top speed, not caring if he flew off the slippery edge to his death.

Above him, he could hear his father's voice, "Nick, wait! Give me a chance to—*Nick!*"

Chase

Nick slowed down when his paws hit the familiar stones of the kitchen floor, but any hope of comfort shattered with his mother's hiss.

"I told him you couldn't do it."

Her words hit Nick like a whip. He leapt for the labyrinth, not stopping until he'd shot out the other end, onto the top step and into the cool dark. Panting, he began the dangerous descent down the Tower wall at a normal walk, dropping stone by stone.

But the slow pace didn't match his racing heart. He wanted instant distance between him and the Tower of his shame.

The clouds shifted, and in the moonlight, Nick saw the gravel walkway a dozen feet below him. Without thinking, he launched himself into the longest leap of his short life.

He landed hard with a crunch of gravel, feeling the impact in every bone. He remained crouched, head bowed for one long moment—plenty long enough to realize his jump had been stupid.

Then the smell hit his nose. He raised his head to discover just how stupid. He looked straight into the glowing eyes of the Tower watchdogs.

Twenty feet away, in the shadow of the Tower guardhouse, two Doberman Pinschers cocked their angular heads in perfect unison. For one heartbeat the three animals stared at each other. Then the dogs were on their feet running at Nick with mad barks, their white fangs glistening in the moonlight. Nick wheeled around and ran for the nearest opening in the courtyard wall, a tall iron gate sixty feet away. He finally streaked through the gate's narrow bars with the Dobermans less than a yard behind him, their barks escalating with frustrated anger. The dogs threw themselves at the gate, stretching their snarling heads through to snap at Nick.

The Tower guard finally caught up, puffing with exertion. "All right, all right that's enough," he commanded. "You'll wake the dead over a cat. Quiet, Antony. I said ENOUGH, Cleo. Sit. NOW!"

From the safety of the street outside, Nick watched the dogs obey, his heart racing. Their voices fell to a whimper, still pleading for the chance to punish him, but the guard dragged them away by their collars. Nick took a deep breath. His heartbeat slowed as he made his way through the Lions Gate and onto the road outside the Tower grounds. He needed a quiet place to clean off the stench of the Tower Ravens.

But now that he was free, he had no idea where to go.

"Bark! Bark! Bark!"

Other dogs had answered the Pinschers' call and taken up the chase. Nick jumped to his feet and raced around the bend in the wide road searching for high ground. He had few options. The Thames River lapped on his right, and the high stone walls of the Tower enclosure blocked him on his left. The few trees nearby were too low to the ground for safety. Nick heard the dogs' voices change. They'd caught his scent.

He sped forward, leaping over piles of rubble in the street, tearing past a few sleepy dockmen and horses preparing for the workday. The dogs were a frenzied pack of six voices baying behind him. They were too close for him to hide. He had to climb.

Nick reached an intersection and turned the corner to head inland. A Great Dane stood sniffing the air at the far end of the street. As the huge animal lunged in his direction, Nick wheeled around to race in the only direction he could go—back toward the river and the end of the dock. The smell of dog overwhelming him, he was reduced to blind panic in a tightening circle of furious barks. Movement overhead caught his eye. Nick looked up. A thick rope for loading boats dangled from a pole extended out over the river. At the edge of the dock, he put all his remaining strength into a leap for the rope's nearest knot.

Nick's world went silent, his concentration narrowed to reaching the rope. He was going to make it!

A sudden gust of wind tugged the rope further from Nick, out over the dark water. He stretched and swam mid-air straining to adjust, but he was already falling. He looked down in terror.

"Bam!"

Nick landed atop the rolling deck of a low river barge. The

wild barks of angry dogs filled his hears again. From his place
behind a thick coil of rope, Nick looked up at the frothing animals fifteen feet above him. The dogs took turns preparing to
leap, but each balked at the long leap over black water.

Nick was safe, but he couldn't stop trembling.

"What's wrong wi' you lot, eh? Shut yer yaps now!" called a
gritty human voice.

Nick's head snapped around at the unexpected sound.

Unaware of Nick, the broad boatman bent over to reach the
forward sail rigging. With the smooth expertise of long practice,
the man unhooked the anchor rope from the ring in the seawall
and raised the brown sail. The barge surged forward beneath
Nick's paws, as the furious dogs slid away.

Nick worked to balance himself against the rock of the vessel
He could only stare, still breathless, as the Tower rose above him
in the dawn light. The Ravens lined the Tower roof, silent and
unmoving, their black eyes boring into his. He knew his father
was up there too, still at work. But Nick couldn't hear or see him.
On the far side of the Tower, he saw his mother sitting atop the
stone wall.

"Mom, go get Dad," he called out to her.

Mona did not move.

"Please!"

Nick's mother looked into his eyes, and then shifted her gaze
to look past him.

Minutes ticked by, and the watery gap between the boat and
the Tower widened with each heartbeat. Nick looked over the
side at the murky water, and then at the high slick walls of the
seawall. Even if he jumped now, he'd never be able to climb out.

When the brown sail puffed with seaward breeze, Mona did
a slow turn, stepped through the crown-shaped hole and melted

into the shadows.

The barge picked up speed and headed for open water.

Nick watched the Tower shrink smaller and smaller, until it vanished.

CHAPTER SEVEN

So Close

In the morning sunlight, Clavier's Beacon looked like any other bronze statue. But Mark knew there was much more to this one, and he stopped sweeping the stone pedestal to look up. Clavier stood above him, the familiar elderly woman with her single braid and smiling face. Yet today, he wanted to know more about her… and about everyone else too. He looked from the red beacon in the statue's right palm to the village clustered in the valley below.

He wanted to know because of what he'd seen right here, last night.

He'd been up and dressed for hours before his father was ready to leave their cottage for the statue this morning. It was the village forester's duty to ensure the beacon burned bright each night and in all weathers to guide travelers to safety in Dreamhaven. Mark watched his father climb the wooden ladder until he was level with the ruby-red oil lamp in Clavier's palm. The lamp's faceted glass dome was eighteen inches across, and he grunted once as he carefully lifted and then placed it in Clavier's free hand.

The sun glinted off the facets, and Mark closed his eyes against the blinding brilliance. The dark instantly reminded him of last night...

·§·

"Mark, Shift, how nice of you to visit," Clavier said, her bronze exterior melting away to reveal a living woman.

"Hi Clavier," Mark said, as Shift dipped his head in greeting.

"That's a lovely skunk torso you're wearing, Shift," she said. "I bet Mark is very glad you're not wearing the smelly end too."

Mark laughed and Shift beamed a toothy grin up at the woman in her long traveling cloak. The red beacon in her palm never wavered as Clavier sat down atop the stone pedestal and beckoned them to join her. Mark draped Shift around his neck and made the climb in a few swift movements. At the top, Shift jumped to Clavier's lap. She stroked his striped head with her free hand.

"So tell me, what brings you two here in middle of the night?"

"I've been thinking about what you said last week," Mark began, "and I don't get how everyone on Earth can have a special dream inside them that's different from anyone else's."

Clavier's nod encouraged him to go on.

"Of course every body is different—"

Clavier and Mark looked down at Shift. He winked one jet-black skunk eye and waved his scaled tail at them.

"—but how can there be enough dreams to go around? Don't most people want the same things?"

Clavier said nothing for several minutes, her eyes focused on a spot in the air about three feet in front of them. Mark and Shift exchanged raised eyebrows. Had they overstepped their friendship with Clavier? Was she angry?

They turned back to her in time to see a six-inch hourglass appear in the air before them. The hourglass floated there, lit from within and emitting a clear steady note.

Mark and Shift leaned forward for a closer look. The bottom half held fine sand, as white as new-fallen snow. In the top half, a three-dimensional object revolved in a slow spin that revealed intricately carved wings painted in bright colors.

"It's a bird," Mark said, surprised that he was whispering. "I've never seen one like it."

One by one, a dozen more hourglasses appeared and hovered in a soft harmony of notes. In the nearest, they could see a spyglass, an exotic flower, a longbow and a crown glinting with diamonds.

"Wow! What are they?" Mark asked.

"They are the answer to your question," Clavier replied.

Shift rattled his tail in approval.

Clavier smiled and patted his scaled back. "Each hourglass holds the symbol for the life dream or goal of someone now living." She gestured toward the decorated bird, with its raised head and open beak. "This symbol belongs to a young girl in Africa who dreams of singing like the songbird that nests outside her window."

Clavier placed her palm beneath a different hourglass that held a bird of prey with spread wings and pieces of seashell embedded in the wood. "This is the dream of a boy your age. He lives in North America, and he hopes to befriend the spirit of an osprey that will show him where to find fish to feed his family."

"Two birds, but really different dreams," Mark said, looking more closely at other hourglasses and their spinning symbols.

"What about this one?" asked Clavier, pointing to the left, "Can you guess anything about this dream?"

Mark and Shift peered at the symbol. The tail and broad flukes of a whale were smooth, and as white as bone. "I've never heard of a white whale," Mark said, looking at Shift, who shook his head. "What does it mean?"

"This is the dream of an American writer nearly 40 years of age. Right now he is writing a truly remarkable story. Perhaps in a few years, he will be famous and you will get the chance to read about his white whale."

For several minutes, the three friends watched the hourglasses amid the quiet song of their combined notes. "But not everyone can be famous, can they?" Mark asked.

"Not everyone wishes to be famous. Many dreams are quiet, yet equal in power and grace to any other."

Mark pointed to another hourglass. "I can't tell what this one is."

"That dream is still very young and has yet to take shape," answered Clavier.

"You mean our life's dream isn't ready when we get it?"

"I mean, that first we have to study ourselves to discover our deepest hopes. Then we and our dreams grow up together, over our whole lives."

"But then how do we know we've got the right dream?"

Clavier winked at Shift. "We pay attention to what makes us smile. We listen to the moments when we feel most content, and we notice what we're doing—and who's there with us."

Mark looked at the floating hourglasses for a long minute. "Do I have a dream symbol?" he asked in a quieter voice.

Clavier's smile deepened.

"Is it one of these? Can I see it?" Mark strained to see more hourglasses, leaning right and left.

"Mark. Mark!"

Mark jumped and opened his eyes as the willow broom clattered to the stones.

His father stood beside him, the ladder at his feet. "You've been standing there with an idle broom for a long time, son," he said. He picked up the ladder and moved toward the shed among the trees. "We won't get any breakfast until we're done, so, please..."

Mark nodded he'd heard and bent down to grab the broom in a tight grip. There was no point letting his father see his frustration. He wouldn't understand. And Mark had no way to explain that last night he'd lost his balance, teetered on the edge and almost fallen off the pedestal. When he'd recovered, the hourglasses were gone, and Shift had stood at Clavier's bronze feet, shaking his head.

Mark kicked at a loose pebble. He'd come so close to seeing his life dream. He wanted to close his eyes and try again right now...

Instead, he went back to sweeping.

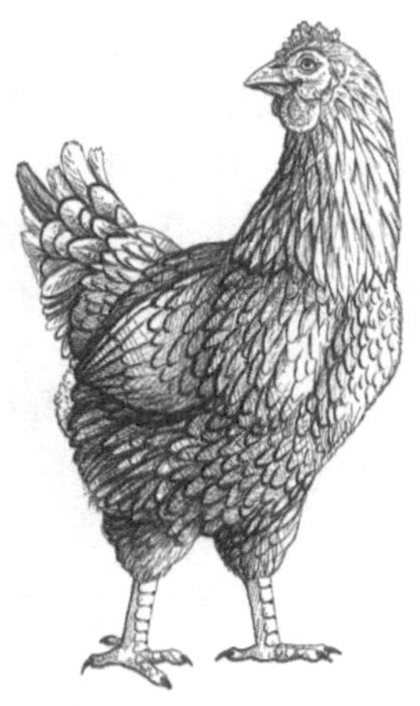

Nick, Meet Smoke

When Nick closed his eyes, one of two things happened: He fell into his lifelong nightmare, or he relived his wretched last night in London. Either way, his sleep was sporadic and fitful.

It had been two long years of hard living since the night of the Ravens, but the painful memories were fresh. He could still hear his father calling his name, the sound echoing down the stone staircase. He thought about going back every day. He'd always planned to go back. But the truth was, he would never be a real cat until he had nine lives. He would never be welcome or accepted anywhere until he could dream like every other cat, or crossover to his other lives another way.

And despite two years of solitary searching, he still hadn't found a way to do either.

So on this soft September night, he was again on the run from the last town, searching for somewhere safe to sleep in a new one. The alley was dark and deserted, a narrow dead end between an apothecary and a feed store. Nick climbed inside a broken crate stuffed with dirty hay. He licked the travel cuts on his paws, but before he could finish, he fell into troubled sleep.

Nick's nose woke him. "Mmmmm, fresh mouse." The blue cat was grateful to escape the clutches of his usual nightmare, but after a week on the run, he didn't have the energy to crack open an eyelid just for a fantasy mouse. Then the delicious scent became undeniable. He stretched out a paw. The mouse was real all right. Maybe he could eat with his eyes closed.

"You look like you could use a good—"

Nick jumped to his feet, fangs bared, defending food he hadn't even seen yet.

"—meal," finished the grey cat.

Rats! Nick had been too distracted by the mouse to pick up the scent of the orange-eyed male sitting three feet away, blocking the alley entrance. Nick dropped into a painful crouch and growled a low challenge. Even to his own ears, there was only one word for the yowl that came out—pathetic. He had to try, but any fool of a cat could see he was in no shape to fight.

"That's really not necessary. I wouldn't have brought a gift if I wanted a fight. I'm Smoke."

Without taking his eyes off the grey, Nick stretched out his left paw and dragged the mouse closer.

"Nick."

His compact benefactor sat up, lifted his right rear paw and licked his toes with casual nonchalance. Nick recognized the attempt to put him at ease. Of course he wasn't going to fall for that, but while the guy was off balance, he might as well eat. He could keep both eyes on "Smoke" while he chewed. The orange-eyed cat watched him eat with quiet patience.

Nick was washing his whiskers when the cat said, "You're different." It wasn't a question. Never was. But at least this cat had let him eat before the fireworks began. Nick decided to try negotiating.

"Look, if you and the others just let me sleep here overnight, I'll leave in the morning."

"Leave? Haven't you just arrived? What 'others'?"

For the first time since he'd smelled the mouse, Nick's curiosity upstaged his exhaustion. He looked into Smoke's fiery eyes looking for the clue that would betray the grey's plan. He sensed nothing suspicious.

"If you're not here to run me out of town, what do you want?"

Smoke crouched down to all fours. "Well, you've obviously been places. And I want to hear about your adventures."

Nick snorted. "Right. My adventures. If you call 'adventures' being chased from more cities, towns and villages than I can remember—then I've got an earful for you." Nick wasn't catching on to the game yet, but he felt certain the trap was about to spring.

Smoke didn't say anything. He sat watching Nick, his head cocked to one side. After a long moment he sat up.

"Okay. Follow me." He turned his back to Nick, and strode toward the mouth of the alley.

Nick's jaw dropped. He didn't get it, first the mouse, and now the invitation. What was this cat up to?

Without stopping, Smoke called over his shoulder, "There'll

be more food at home. Rose is out hunting too."

Nick didn't move from his spot. He wanted to think. If this was a trap, it had been stupid to feed him and let him regain some strength. But then, that wouldn't matter if a gang were waiting to jump him at the end of the alley. He sniffed the air. Nothing. But they could be hiding downwind.

Smoke turned right at the alley entrance and was out of sight when Nick heard him say, "You'll want to meet Rose. She's a dreamdancer."

A dreamdancer! Smoke had Nick's full attention now. It might be a trap, but this guy was good. Dreamdancers were rare and revered cats. So rare that Nick had assumed they were a myth.

Normal cats easily traveled time and space through their personal dreams. But legend said that a dreamdancer could travel the dreams of other cats. Any cat. Nick had never believed he'd meet a living, breathing dreamdancer, but if Smoke knew one, maybe she could help him.

He creaked to his feet and pulled a long stretch, working to keep his groans to himself. He caught up with Smoke behind the butcher shop. The thick smells ran from disgusting to delicious, and Nick's hunger brought him to a stop. In France, he'd shared the long, lonely hours of a night watchman at a train bridge, and the man had eased Nick's hunger with generous bits from his nightly meatloaf sandwich. In Spain, the crippled daughter of the township judge was known to secretly pour her evening cream into a porcelain jewelry box left on the windowsill. If he was lucky, Smoke lived here at the butcher's.

But the grey cat kept walking. Nick took a longing sniff and fell back into step beside Smoke. They crossed two more silent streets and then turned left. Still on high alert, Nick kept his nose working, and shifted his head from side to side scanning for hidden attackers.

"Rose is…?" Nick began, but stopped, feeling he'd already given too much away with his interest.

"My sister. And yes, she really is a dreamdancer," Smoke answered easily, a grin breaking over his lips.

And that's when Nick knew Smoke had seen his real hunger—the one that had nothing to do with food.

CHAPTER NINE

Smoke's Family

The stars were fading to dawn when Nick and Smoke stepped through a white iron gate into a modest garden brimming with fall flowers. Nick followed Smoke to a white cottage, the stones of the footpath gritty beneath his paws. Green shutters flanked two windows on either side of the wooden door. The house sat dark and quiet. Smoke hopped up three steps to the wooden porch with an air of ownership.

"Usually we go in through the cellar and up through a hole in the laundry room, but it's been so warm we can use the front window tonight," Smoke said. "If you'll wait here just a second,

I'll tell Rose we have company."

Nick nodded once, cool and casual, but as soon as Smoke jumped onto the window ledge, Nick retraced his steps to the gate: He'd have a better view of the house and a shorter escape route from there.

"That's not necessary either," Smoke called over his shoulder as he dropped inside.

Moments later, a female cat appeared at the window, nose pressed to the glass.

"Come on in," Smoke called. "I promise no one will jump you."

Nick started forward, but veered left and headed for the back of the cottage. He made it a rule never to take the expected route. He continued past the vegetable garden, and climbed three stone steps to a screen door propped open for cooling breezes. He peered into the tiny kitchen. The smell of food, humans and felines was a rich mix. What he didn't smell was anything unexpected. He stepped inside just as Smoke and his sister padded into view.

Smoke rolled his eyes at Nick, but when he made the introductions, he seemed amused, and maybe even a little proud of Nick's cagey detour. "Rose, meet Nick—now that he's decided to come inside."

Nick knew the polite response was to relax and do a little grooming to show he was friendly. But he wasn't ready for that, so he sat on his haunches and told his tail to lie calm. In case the two siblings really were as welcoming as they appeared, he didn't want to risk an insult with a surly tail.

Rose had huge green eyes rimmed in black, and what she lacked in weight, she made up for in fur. Even in early fall, her coat was thick gray with touches of salmon on her back and sides. Her ruff, paws and underbelly were pure white, and she had matching tufts of white fur in her ears.

Nick relaxed a notch. Now that he'd met Rose, he felt he could easily win if a fight broke out. And he was intrigued. Like her brother, Rose wasn't showing any of the familiar responses to him: instant dislike and spitting anger. She crossed to Nick, and reached her nose forward to sniff him, an invitation for him to do the same. When he responded, Rose's purr erupted, impossibly loud for such a small cat. Nick smiled despite his desire to remain in control of the situation.

"Welcome, Nick," said Rose in a rich voice.

Nick sat stunned in the rising glow of dawn. Welcome? "Welcome" was new territory for Nick. These two were either great pretenders, or they were genuinely the friendliest cats he'd ever met.

"It's a pleasure to meet such a rare cat," Rose continued, indicating Nick's blue-tinged fur.

"A dreamdancer is rare. I'm unheard of." said Nick, flashing a wicked smile that relaxed the siblings.

Smoke seemed to take his sister's reaction as confirmation that Nick was okay to stay. "So let's eat," he said, grinning back. "I'm starving."

All three cats heard the creak of bedsprings and a human step in the bedroom, but Nick was the only one that bolted out the screen door.

"It's okay," Smoke called. "It's Adele, our human."

"She's safe. You'll see," added Rose. Nick retraced his path to the garden as far as the lowest step, and waited, upright and ready to run. A few moments later, a woman stepped into sight. She had two long braids of brown hair and kind eyes the same color. Her face looked smooth and unlined, and she moved with the ease of a young, but adult human.

"Good morning, my loves," she whispered, reaching down to pet Smoke and Rose, who were weaving figure eights through her legs and over her slippers. Smiling, she stepped toward the sink, but stopped when she caught sight of Nick perched on the bottom step.

"Well, who have we here?" Her voice was soft and even, and she asked as if she really wanted to know. She leaned forward to get a better look at Nick. "You look like you've seen some miles, friend," she whispered.

Without thinking, Nick meowed in response. Adele smiled, and then looked from Nick to Smoke and Rose.

"Well, it seems you three have already worked things out. Would you like to come in and have a meal?" she asked, pushing the door wider for Nick.

·§·

"No! No! No! I won't have it, Adele," the man's voice boomed through the cottage from the parlor, where Adele and her husband were arguing. Bart looked at least a decade older than Adele, and his face held none of her kindness.

It had been five days since Nick's arrival. The three felines were crouched in a row beneath the bed, eyes wide, ears pitched forward, watching the humans from the safety of the bedroom across the hall.

"Bart, I'm right here. There's no need to yell," Adele said in a soft, but firm voice.

"Well, you don't seem to hear what I'm saying otherwise," Bart said at full volume, "not when it comes to those cats. It was bad enough I had to take the two you brought with you when we married. But I am not takin' in a stray. This is my home, not a flophouse for fleabags."

"Fleabags! He's the one always scratchin'," Nick whispered to Rose and Smoke. "Maybe if he groomed a little he wouldn't reek."

"And you haven't even smelled the worst yet," said Smoke.

Bart picked up a woodchip and flung it into the fire. A shower of sparks flew up. He turned back to Adele. "I work hard to put food on the table, and I'm not gonna' add another mouth."

"He's barely lifted a finger since I've been here. Does he even work?" Nick asked.

Smoke answered. "We wondered the same thing, so I followed him for a week. Turns out he rents out his old family farm—some outbuildings and several plots of land outside town. He seems the worst kind of landlord. I saw him evict a family from a shack that was practically falling down. They'd asked him to replace the broken glass in the only window they had."

"I'm not surprised," said Nick. "But I don't know why he's so riled up about food. He's not the one I left hungry."

Rose and Smoke pulled their eyes from the humans long enough to smile at Nick.

He'd been slow to catch on about food in the house. The third morning, soon after breakfast, he'd seen Rose drop a mouse in front of Smoke in the back garden. Nick was ashamed. He'd been wolfing down what Adele put in their dish, and neither of the others had had a bite of the easy food since he'd arrived. But unlike Bart, they hadn't said a word. That same afternoon, Nick had dropped a fresh catch at the feet of each cat, and sauntered away to the sound of happy purrs.

"Bart, you know I feed the cats scraps and discards we don't want."

The three cats glanced at each other. That was mostly true but sometimes there were tender bits of chicken or fish from

Adele's plate hidden beneath the scraps.

That was another thing Nick had learned. Adele adored her cats. And he understood that she welcomed him, as long as Smoke and Rose were happy. He'd noticed right away that the woman was content in the company of the felines, but she tensed whenever Bart entered a room.

"Two is two cats too many. Besides, you already treat them better than you treat me."

"Bart, you know that's not true. I do my best to make you happy. And the cats do their part too. They keep the house free of mice and other rodents. And the other night the stray fought off a raccoon that had Rose pinned."

"Well…he's creepy with that blue fur. I don't like the way he looks at me."

"'Creepy' huh?" Nick growled. "If only you could see how I'm looking at you now." He didn't like Bart. The man smelled of anger and slyness.

Adele's laugh seemed a little forced, but Bart didn't seem to notice. "Well 'that creepy blue one' is an extremely rare breed," she said. "Someone must be frantic to have lost him."

"If only," Nick mumbled to himself.

"I'm surprised you think he notices us at all. Trust me. That one will move on any day now. We'll turn around, and he'll be gone," Adele finished.

Rose and Smoke looked at Nick, but he avoided their gaze. He didn't want to give away his disappointment. He hoped Adele was just placating Bart, and that she didn't really want him to leave. Because truth was, he wasn't keen to go. He liked having a safe place to sleep and a daily routine. But he most enjoyed something he'd never had before—friends.

And he was still studying Rose to find out all he could about this dreamdancer thing. She usually seemed like a perfectly normal cat, and she was wicked smart. Pleasant, if a little serious, Rose enjoyed Smoke's tales from town, but she rarely left the house in search of her own fun.

Smoke nudged Nick, bringing him back to the present. "In a minute, he'll forget all about kicking you out, just watch."

Adele spoke soothingly to Bart. "Why don't I make you a nice roast duck tonight? You can have the whole thing to yourself."

Bart had his back to Adele and the cats, but they could see he listened. "Well, that'd be a start. Maybe," he said in a sulky voice.

Smoke rolled his eyes at Nick and Rose. At least Bart wasn't yelling anymore.

"And I've got some fresh apples from the tree. Would you like me to make you a pie?"

"Yeah, with that cinnamon sauce you make."

"Consider it done. Why don't you curl up in your chair and take a nice nap." Adele rose from her seat by the fire to steer Bart to his favorite chair. She draped the green wool blanket over his legs.

"When you wake up, I'll have a nice dinner waiting for you."

"And those cats won't get a single bite," Bart flared.

"He's a nasty piece of work," Rose whispered.

But Nick and Smoke scrunched their faces, mocking Bart's bitter words, until Rose was giggling. This storm had blown over.

When Parents Disagree

I don't think this is the best choice for Mark," Minette said, rising from her treadle sewing machine to take a seat in the chair opposite her husband and the crackling fire. A low shaft of late November sunlight illuminated the gap between husband and wife, and both knew Mark would arrive home any minute. "He's young—just eleven years old," Minette continued. "There's still plenty of time, years and years for him to learn from you. Forcing Mark to leave school too early could backfire. Maybe, if you waited another year, he would willingly choose to be a forester."

"Of course he'll choose the forest," Sean said. "My family

have worked and tended trees for generations. It's a good livelihood and a valuable skill. You know that."

"I do know. But Mark—"

"I've made up my mind." Sean hated to ruin one of her good days with an argument. But if he didn't tell her now, he'd feel he'd deceived her.

A red flush climbed from Minette's neck to her face. "This isn't your decision alone," she said in a quiet voice.

Sean turned away, and reached for his pipe, wishing he'd never started the conversation.

Minette softened her tone. "Why can't there be room for Mark to follow his own heart—and dreams?"

Sean's frustration spilled over in a rush of words. "Because he's lost in the dreams of a child, a fantasy world of talking animals and endless adventure. The sooner he understands the real world, the sooner he'll begin to pull his weight for the family and the village."

Minette sat up straighter. "Mark 'pulls his weight' now with his chores. And he's already helping the village by teaching some of the younger children. He's wonderful with them."

"It's time he learned his craft."

Minette reached out, placing her hand on his arm. "Sean, please don't let what's happening to me rob Mark of his childhood. Mark's dreams are his hope—who knows where they can lead him? Let's give him a little more time to find out."

"I know I'm right about this. I need Mark right here, firmly planted in reality. His constant slips into another world aren't right!" Sean regretted the words as soon as he'd said them. At the sound of footsteps approaching the cottage, they both fell silent.

·§·

"I'm home" Mark called from the mudroom, closing the cottage door against the cold. He shed the protection of hat, muffler and mittens, dropped his wool-lined boots in the corner to dry and stepped into the main room. His father sat, barely visible over the high back of his comfortable chair, staring into the fire. His mother stood at her sewing machine, bending low over a bright dress, a Christmas gift for Angela Del'arte. But Mark didn't need to see their faces to know he'd interrupted a conversation he wasn't meant to hear. His body tingled with the tension in the air.

In the past, Mark had always looked forward to arriving home after school. The steep climb up the snow-covered hill had usually ended with a hot fire dancing in the grate, his mother's welcoming smile, and a thick wedge of her spice cake. Sometimes his father had already arrived home, and together the family would settle into their evening routine and a delicious meal.

But this winter, Minette's memory lapses meant Mark never knew what to expect when he opened the door. He could find his mother stirring a bubbling pot of hearty stew. Or standing in the middle of the cold room, baffled by the yellow onion in her hand.

He was glad she was having a good day today.

"Welcome home," she said, crossing to him.

Mark wrapped his mother in a fierce bear hug. He'd grown two inches over the last year and they were now the same height. Over her shoulder, he smiled at his father, who waved a tight welcome. Mark could feel his mother's love flow into him as she laughed and motioned him toward the wood-burning stove. "There's warm cocoa in the pan," she smiled.

Mark grabbed the kitchen towel with one hand, and a metal

mug from the shelf with the other. Whatever had caused the tension between his parents, he could already sense them relaxing. They all wanted to enjoy the month leading up to Christmas.

As he sipped his hot chocolate, Mark thought of the Christmas gifts hidden in his loft room. He'd started making his father's last July, and this week he'd finally finished: A walking staff carved with four wrap-around figures, one for each season of the year. For spring Mark had chosen an eagle, young wings spread in the joy of flight. Summer was an upright bear pulling ripe berries from a branch. Mark had carved a stag in mid-leap for fall. But winter had been the easiest choice, and the most challenging: Father Christmas. Mark smiled. The staff had come out very much as he'd pictured it in his mind. Maybe for once his "over-imagination" would please his father.

And his mother's gift remained the one good memory he'd brought home from Les Contamines.

Last summer, when his mother's mind had begun to wander too often, the family had traveled five days over the mountains to the nearest doctor. His eyes had been kind as he listened to Minette describe her increasing bouts of confusion and shifts into the past, but he'd sent them on to the clinic in Les Contamines.

There, his mother and father awakened each day at dawn and departed for the clinic early, leaving Mark in the care of the owner of the small hotel, Mme. Soleil. Though he never expected them back before evening, waiting was hard. He tried to distract himself by working on new drawings of Shift and he defending Dreamhaven against flying serpents. But, one day at noon, Mme. Soleil found him pacing in the garden, an incomplete sketch abandoned on the table.

"Mark, you are a very good artist for one so young," she said, her grey eyes kind. "I think you would enjoy drawing our beautiful river. It's only a short walk away, and I have to pass there to shop for fruit for tonight's dinner. Why don't we go to the river together, then you'll know the way back."

She packed him a sandwich of cheese and sweet pickles on crusty bread, and he ate it on a wooden bench in the shade beside the river. He'd been drawing for over an hour when an elderly man and woman approached him.

"My name is Alicia and this is my husband Martine. We've been watching you sketch from the bridge down there," the woman pointed. "May we see your drawing?"

The couple's interest seemed genuine, so Mark re-opened the cover of the sketchpad he'd closed.

"This is beautifully done," said Alicia.

"Just as we'd hoped," nodded her husband. "What is your name, young man?"

"Mark Farrallon, sir."

"Mark, would you be willing to draw us just there at the water's edge? We'd like to take a picture home to remind us of our visit. I will, of course, pay you for your work."

Mark often daydreamed about being an illustrator of fine books like the ones his teacher, Mr. Wolfram, lent him. And he'd had lots of practice drawing figures from his dreams.

"Yes, sir, I think I can do that for you," he answered.

Half an hour later, Alicia and Martine were delighted with their picture, and Mark had become the proud owner of a gold coin. The couple had taken Mark along with them to the framers, where Mark traded his new coin for a delicate oval frame ten inches tall. The frame, edged with fine black velvet, also had a border of hand-painted gold.

He returned to the hotel and was surprised to find his parents already there. From their strained faces, he knew what they were going to say: The doctors could offer no cure. His family left for home the next morning, determined to enjoy Minette's good days—and cope with the hard ones.

Once he was back in Dreamhaven, Mark had begun to draw from a childhood memory of his mother smiling in front of the cottage, a basket of fresh flowers on her arm. Mark worked many hours to capture the contentment he'd seen on her face that spring morning.

Now the picture was finished and mounted in the frame from Les Contamines, and at least once a day, Mark pulled back the soft tissue wrapping to check on his gift. He couldn't wait to give it to his mother.

Fortified with hot cocoa, and thoughts of Christmas, Mark made quick work of his chores. He stoked the fire with logs from the woodpile outside, and refilled the massive water jug with clean snow, setting it to melt on the hearth. Once he'd laid the dinner table and helped his mother put potatoes in the stove to bake, he sat down beside the fire and took out his notebook.

Writing the last chapter of "Two Swords Beneath Timbuktu" would be the perfect way to stop worrying about his parents' argument.

Rose
and the Rabbit

Nick and Smoke were lying in the garden in a puddle of rare November sun.

"…so that's Paris—fat, tasty rats and lots of bridges," finished Nick. Smoke lay with a dreamy look in his orange eyes.

Nick lay beside Smoke, content to drift into easy silence. Relaxing around any cat other than his father was a new experience for Nick, and he felt grateful. He'd come to think of Smoke as "The Gentleman Cat." The grey was kind without being wimpy; a deadly hunter, yet merciful to his prey, and he was fiercely loyal to his sister. Smoke was a great listener and endlessly curious about Nick's "adventures," but he didn't talk much about himself. Nick decided to ask some questions of his own.

"Smoke, I don't get your wanderlust."

"What do you mean?" Smoke asked, grooming his left shoulder with long vigorous licks.

"Don't you have plenty of adventures in your other lives?"

Smoke kept grooming as if Nick hadn't spoken.

Nick had the feeling Smoke was avoiding the question. Despite his even greater curiosity, he let several moments pass, and then said in a nonchalant voice, "So what about it? Why don't you just spend more time in your more exciting lives?"

Smoke's answer came slowly, "Because…this is my favorite life, and…" Smoke returned to grooming his fur.

"And…?" Nick prompted.

"And this is the only life I share with Rose." Smoke's tail started to switch slowly from side to side. Nick had no idea why Smoke would be agitated.

"But your sister happens to be the only living dreamdancer anyone has ever heard of. She's the one cat that can enter any cat's dreams. Why can't Rose just join you in another life?"

"It doesn't work that way." Smoke said through a tight jaw.

"Well, okay, then, let's stick to this life. If you're so keen to travel, why haven't you just taken off?"

Smoke looked at Nick, but said nothing, so Nick tried a new approach. "Well, I know Rose and Adele would miss you, but you're not getting any younger. You should hit the road while you can."

"I'm needed here," Smoke said, shrugging to dismiss further questions.

"I agree that you're loved and well-fed, but needed may be a little strong. Lots of tomcats take off to see the world before they settle down. I'm sure Rose would understand." When Smoke didn't respond, Nick dropped his tone and looked Smoke right in the eyes with a new sympathy he'd never before felt—let alone voiced to another cat.

"Believe me, I'd understand if you're, you know, a little nervous. It's a big world out there and—"

Smoke leapt to his feet. Nick had never seen him angry before, but Smoke was fuming, no question. Nick rose to his feet in response.

"It's not the world out there. It's the one here. Bart can't be trusted. When Rose and Adele choose another home, I'll go. But not before." The grey cat turned his back and stalked from the garden.

Nick stood rooted to his spot, stunned by Smoke's words. He didn't know the best way to talk to his friend right now, so he decided not to go after him. But he did know, that from now on, he would keep a closer eye on Bart.

Later that afternoon, Nick returned from a scouting expedition to find Smoke crouched on the path to the backyard, watching Rose and a small rabbit. Rose sat nose to nose with the cottontail, staring into its red eyes. Nick crouched down beside Smoke. "Wow! Is Rose hypnotizing him for the kill?" he whispered.

"No, she's helping him."

"Helping him what, fatten up?"

"No. It's part of Rose being a dreamdancer…I can't explain. You'll have to ask her."

"Yeah, I will. Right after I make that rabbit our dinner." Nick crouched to crawl forward.

Smoke rose to his feet, barring Nick's path.

"The rabbit's under Rose's protection."

Nick matched Smoke's height and looked into the grey's eyes to see if he was joking.

"And mine," Smoke added.

Nick dropped back to a crouch, signaling he'd heard. "Okaaaay, if you say so."

"You can add it to your list of questions for Rose, but the rabbit goes free." Smoke's tone was still charged with challenge.

"You have my word, so drop it." Nick hated to see perfectly good meat go to waste, and his own tone said so.

Smoke dropped beside Nick. "Sorry, I just needed you to understand."

Nick sensed Smoke's disappointment that they'd clashed again. The whole thing was weird, but Nick decided he wasn't going to hold a grudge against Smoke over one lost meal.

"Well I don't understand, but heck, if it's that important to you and Rose, I'll help you protect him."

Smoke grinned, and they sat in silence until the rabbit gave a quiver, hopped across the yard and disappeared in the grass outside the south fence. Rose came to her feet slowly. She looked toward Smoke and Nick, but her eyes were distant and unfocused. As the male cats followed her into the house, Nick had some serious doubts about his chances of getting fat as long as he lived with a dreamdancer.

CHAPTER TWELVE

Nick's Message

Rose and Nick sat side-by-side in the front room window seat, enjoying the warmth of the December fire. From there they could see the ice sculptures on the front porch. Adele had carved all three cat faces into a single ice block, and they were excellent likenesses. Nick felt pleased that his was quite handsome. Across the room, Bart snored like a two-ton bear, his chair pulled up close to the grate. From the kitchen, they could hear Adele washing the dishes, and Smoke's contented meows as he kept her company.

Nick appeared to be in a light doze. But his insides were a

twitching mess. He had the perfect chance to talk to Rose, a dreamdancer, and probably the only one he'd ever meet. Maybe she could fix his nightmare. Or maybe she could get him to his other lives another way. Or maybe…who knew what was possible if she worked her magic?

But he let the frost-kissed night slip by in silence. Much as he wanted to trust Rose, there were lots of reasons Nick felt wary.

First of all, Rose was spooky. And Nick had already experienced Rose's eerie gift once. Late the night he'd met Rose, Nick had looked into her eyes and felt like he'd dropped into an infinite green waterfall. Unnerved, Nick had been the one to break eye contact. Since he'd gotten to know her, he'd never felt that way again. But he hadn't looked into her eyes much either. Rose was uncanny in other ways too. All felines communicated with subtle tail and ear flicks, bumps, nips and licks. But Rose read cats and other animals as if she were privy to a secret language. Way too often she seemed to respond to what he was thinking, instead of what he said.

"Nick, if I can, I'd like to help you with your dreams," said Rose.

She'd done it again. Nick looked away without responding. He knew that once he started THE conversation, Rose would know more about him than anyone. His entire-humiliating-one-and-only life would be exposed. And when Rose told Smoke, he'd lose the only friends he'd ever had and…

"I'm sorry. I didn't mean to be rude."

Nick turned to Rose. "No, it's okay. I want to tell you. Well, ask you, sort of—" He decided to start over. "Maybe you could answer some questions first about, you know, your 'gift'."

Rose studied him for what seemed like minutes, and Nick felt just about ready to call the whole thing off, when she finally spoke. "Of course I'll try to answer your questions. But even though we've heard about dreamdancers from the time we were kittens, I've never met another one. I've learned a little about my 'gift' as you call it from cat lore handed down through generations. But most of what I know I've learned through trial and error and trusting my own instincts."

It hadn't occurred to Nick that Rose didn't know everything about her special talent. He decided to ask his questions anyway. "Okay, so what about that rabbit last month? And the doe last week?"

"The rabbit asked me to travel in dream to tell his warren leader why he'd been gone from home so long. And the deer asked me to…"

Nick's jaw fell open in shock. "You can travel the dreams of other animals besides cats?"

Rose nodded. "I often deliver messages between those who can't reach each other the normal ways."

"So you can enter any animal's dream? That's…amazing. That's great!" Nick's mind raced. He stopped when Rose sighed and looked away. "What, Rose?"

"You wanted to know about the doe." At Nick's nod, she went on, her eyes distant with memory. "She asked me to look in dream for her lost fawn." Rose looked at Nick, her next words a whisper. "I searched many days for her baby's dreams. But there were none, and…" Rose's voice trailed off, and she shuddered.

"I…I'm sorry, Rose," Nick wasn't sure how to comfort her. This conversation hadn't gone at all as he'd expected. He wanted to ask Rose to teach him how to dream like other cats. But it hadn't occurred to him that dreamdancing might bring her pain. He assumed everyone else always had wonderful dreams.

"It's okay, Nick. Keep asking your questions."

"You sure?" When Rose nodded he went on. "Okay. Don't take this the wrong way, but if you're a real dreamdancer, how come I've never heard of you?"

Rose smiled. That's one of the traditions handed down for ages: Dreamdancers don't make a big deal about their gift. But we do try to use it for those who ask for our help."

"That's perfect!" Nick blurted. "I mean—you know I can't get to my other lives, but based on what you're saying—" Nick paused, strangely shy to say what he'd been thinking, now that the chance had come.

"Yes?" Rose prompted.

"What if we tried to visit my other lives together? Maybe after that, I'd be able to dream over on my own." There, he'd said it. He'd asked for her help.

Rose sat silent for an eternity. When she spoke, he heard sympathy in her voice. Or was it pity?

"If I could, of course I'd try that. But dreams aren't like that."

Nick could taste the first ashy hint of disappointment on his tongue. "How does it work then?" he asked, an edge in his voice.

"Each of our nine lives is a part of us. They only exist because we inhabit them. Without you, your lives are just...possibilities waiting to become real. I can't go there until you bring them to life."

Nick jolted in panic. "How long can my other lives exist without me? Will they die if I don't get there soon? Are they dying now?"

Rose closed her eyes. When she reopened them, she answered in a quieter voice. "I just tried to find out the answer to your questions in dream. But no answer arose. I wish I knew, Nick, but I don't."

Nick looked away to hide his frustration and anger. His life was even more messed up than he'd thought.

"What I do know," said Rose, "is that time works differently in each of our nine lives. And each world ceases to exist when we leave there for the last time—when we die in that world."

"Great. That's just great. My lives could die before I ever reach them. Deaths 9, Lives 1— " Nick stopped, stunned by another thought. "What if I've already died in all my other lives, and I just don't remember?"

"You would remember, I've asked enough cats to know that for sure."

"Well, I guess that's good news. But it doesn't matter. I can't get to my other lives, so they may as well be dead." He turned away from Rose.

"Nick, I'm the only dreamdancer we know of, and you're the first cat any of us has ever heard of with this…challenge. I can't believe it's a coincidence that we've met."

Nick's laugh came out short and bitter. If Rose only knew how much he'd believed she was the answer to his problems, how desperately he'd been hoping…

"I think I can still help," Rose continued. "We just have to find the right way. Why don't you show me exactly what happens when you go to sleep, begin to dream and start your journey?"

Nick had been longing to show Rose exactly that. But now he paused, uncertain. Every time he went to sleep, his nightmare terrified him and left him shaking and weak. Now that he knew Rose might be vulnerable, could he ask her to risk that?

All his life he'd just wanted to reach his other lives and become a normal cat. And since the night he'd met Smoke and Rose, he'd dared to imagine the moment Rose stepped into his nightmare and made his life right.

But Rose wasn't even sure she could help him. What if she

tried and failed—just like all the other fixes he'd tried in the past? Nick shuddered. Rose was his friend, and probably his last chance to become normal. But he wanted to think about what she'd said, and try to prepare for disappointment.

The fire had burned to low embers by the time Nick made up his mind. He wouldn't expose Rose to his nightmare. Or at least not yet. But she might have shown him how to get something else he'd wanted for two long years. "Rose, would you be willing to take a message to my father?"

If the green-eyed dreamdancer was surprised by Nick's new direction, she didn't let on. "Absolutely."

"So how do we start?" Nick asked.

"First, you give me specific information about your father to help me find him in dream. You can tell me his name, and where he might be in this world, if you've any idea. And what he looks like would help too. I can use those facts as a sort of…trail for me to follow and find him most quickly."

"Well that's easy. My father's name is Byron. He's a strapping tabby, and he's famous in catdom, because he's the Guardian of the Tower Ravens. And how about this for a trail marker? He lives and works in a grand stone building in London, England. You can't miss it."

Nick laughed. He'd grown more and more excited thinking about his father. Without realizing it, he'd come to his feet, his tail rippling.

Rose smiled. "Well he does seem easy to find. Now what's your message? What should I tell your father when I find him?"

"Oh, right…um." The memory of his fateful last night in London and the final words between him and his father ricocheted through Nick, draining away his enthusiasm. He sat back down. Over and over, he'd imagined what he would say if he ever had the chance. But now he wouldn't be the one talking to his father. Still, Rose was the next best thing, and Nick had a lot he wanted to say.

"Tell him I got chased off the dock and landed on a boat and I couldn't—but I tried—" Nick broke off. He took a deep breath and pictured his dad.

There was plenty to say, but only a few words that really mattered. "Tell him I'm okay…that I'm sorry…and I miss him." Nick was done, but he couldn't look at Rose.

CHAPTER THIRTEEN

Sean's Plan

Mark paused to watch a woodpecker that had landed on the bare branch over his head. In the fading, December light, the bird's black-and-white speckled chest seemed bright.

"By the time I was your age," Mark's father said over his shoulder, "I'd already been working in the woods with my father for a full season."

Mark sometimes enjoyed working beside his father, but tonight he didn't know where the conversation was going, and his stomach had already balled into a tight knot. The woodpecker gave him a sidelong look as if in sympathy, before flying into the quiet safety of the deeper forest.

Mark bent to choose another log from the low sled, and wrestled it over to his father, who lifted it into place atop the growing woodpile in the shed. The heavy work might have been enough excuse for Mark's mute nods, but physical effort wasn't really the reason for his silence.

"Son, you've always been a dreamer. Sometimes your head's so far in the clouds with your imaginary friends—" His father took a breath. "What I'm saying is that dreams won't ever put food on the table. And all this daydreaming…it's just not healthy."

Mark opened his mouth to respond, but his father wasn't looking at him. He forged on, oblivious.

"I've been patient, and gone along with you staying in school, but—"

Mark had pulled the last, thick log from the sled, and he handed it off to his father, who paused to heft it into place. Then he held the wooden doors closed, as Mark dropped the carved bar that secured them in place. Their firewood sat protected for the remaining winter months.

When his father draped a sweaty arm over his shoulders, Mark turned to see if he could read his father's expression, but his face was turned away, eyes fixed on the back door of the cottage. Mark knew his mother was inside making dinner. His father leaned toward him, speaking low.

"I've been more than patient. And now, come spring, you'll be leaving school to become a forester like your ol' dad and his father before him and so on, way back in time. Then you'll find that real trees and a good day's work are more satisfying than any dream. Some friend you've got, you can't even touch him."

Mark almost doubled over. He felt like he'd been hit in the

stomach with a thick tree branch.

His father moved to the wooden bench beside the door and bent to unlace his right boot. As he dropped the second boot, he looked up into Mark's face.

"I promise you, as a forester, you'll always have the respect of the villagers. There's not going to be any more talk of you being a writer, an artist or a teacher, so don't go bothering your mother with this. The decision's final, and you'll see, son, it's for the best."

His father stood, unlatched the door and stepped into the cottage. "Minette, you've got two hungry men on your hands," he called. The door swung shut and latched with a soft "click."

Mark stood staring at the carved door, until his knees buckled, plopping him to the wooden plank. He peeled his deerskin gloves from his hands and sat staring at them, but blind.

His father had been wrong about at least one thing. Mark wasn't hungry.

Heart-to-Heart

Mark's desk sat closest to the roaring schoolhouse hearth, and the heat wasn't helping his struggle to stay awake through Ancient History, his final lesson of the day. Mr. Wolfram's voice seemed to be coming through a long narrow tube.

"…and in 539, the Persian king, Cyrus the Great, conquers Babylon and…"

And then Mr. Wolfram was gone, and Shift was sprawled beside Mark atop a massive log on the river's shady bank. The summer day simmered, but the snow-fed river made Mark's dangling feet ache. Shift had the upper body of a bobcat, and as he listened to Mark, he tracked the darting flight of a blue dragonfly.

"…so I don't know what to do. Do you think my father is right? Do you think I should give up dreaming and our adventures because they're bad for me?" Mark finished.

Shift remained silent so long that he tried again.

"Why would my father tell me my dreams are bad for me if they aren't?"

"Fear," Shift answered, eyes still on the dragonfly.

Mark snorted. "Fear? What fear?"

"Fear that he can't control your fate any more than your mother's. Fear that you'll change and become someone or something he can't understand—or be close to."

Mark's jaw had dropped open, but at Shift's words he closed it in slow consideration. He had never imagined his father afraid of anything. The man could stay in the deep forest for days, alone among prowling predators, and return carefree and smiling.

"That's just crazy."

Shift turned to look at Mark. "You're his only son. And now he's especially afraid because your mom is ill."

"If he's so worried about losing me, why did he go without even saying good—" Mark couldn't continue.

Shift said nothing, but he gazed at Mark with sympathetic golden eyes. He resumed washing his right foot to give Mark a chance to recover.

"In humans, fear runs deep and it's slow to die." he said. Shift waggled his ears and whiskers. "Take for example how they think about cats."

Mark spluttered. "Are you telling me you think humans still believe cats are evil?"

"No, I'm saying that it wouldn't take much to convince some people that cats are self-centered, don't like humans and aren't to be trusted."

"Well, maybe…okay, but—" Mark felt uncomfortable. "I had another question, but now I'm not sure I want to ask you."

"Aaah, come on, ask me another one," Shift teased.

Mark took a deep breath, and then let it out all at once. "Okay…" he tried, but he couldn't make his voice sound nonchalant. "I've been wondering…what would happen—between you and me—if I didn't dream for a while? Would you…disappear?" Mark's question ended in a whisper.

Shift rolled to his feet, dug his claws into the log and arched his scaled back in a lazy stretch. Then he jumped to the grassy bank, and sat looking up into Mark's blue eyes. Mark smiled despite his worry. Shift was so darn fun to watch.

"Clavier promised that if we helped each other, our dreams would always be beautiful and inspiring," Shift began. "I think you and I share your best, most inspiring dreams. I think we should trust Clavier. In fact, I think we should—"

Suddenly Mark and Shift were floating beneath the surface of the river. Sunlight dappled their skin and flowed over the river otters playing tag beside them. The skin-numbing water was suddenly warm and comfortable.

Shift positioned himself nose-to-nose with Mark and looked into the boy's eyes. "Even when you leave dream, I'm never far away. And whenever you return to dream, I'll be waiting for you."

Though they were both underwater, Shift's words rang clear and strong in Mark's ears. He felt the knot in his chest dissolve, and he knew he was grinning like a fool.

Shift rolled onto his back. "Last one to the bridge kisses Dempsey," he called, as he shot downstream.

Mark's forehead smacked the desktop. He startled awake and

pulled himself upright. All his friends were laughing at him.

"And on that note, I think we'll end class for today," Mr. Wolfram said with mock severity.

Mark flushed red with embarrassment. But as he headed up the hill toward home, he remembered Shift's comforting words. He whistled as he crested the hill.

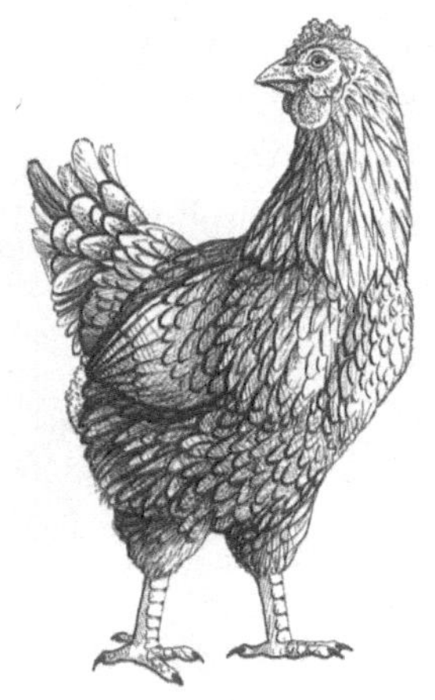

CHAPTER FIFTEEN

Dreamdancer

Rose closed her eyes. In an instant she was walking the path that always began her dreamdances, and she was grateful for the familiar transition. She knew where she was headed, and she smiled in anticipation of her first stop on the journey to deliver Nick's message.

Despite constant searching in each of her nine lives, the green-eyed cat had never discovered another living dreamdancer. But she had found help to safely use the strange gift she'd had since birth.

In dream, Rose arrived at a stone temple atop a sun-drenched hill. She crossed beneath the high entry arch and continued through twelve vast chambers to the heart of the building. The black Goddess of Cats lounged on a throne of soft moss. Even in this languid pose, Bast's power was unquestionable. Five times Rose's size, she was lithe and all muscle. Her presence filled the room without effort. The Goddess looked at Rose with eyes that were golden crescent moons.

"Mother Bast," Rose sent her unspoken greeting as a feeling.

"Daughter," the Cat Goddess sent back.

"I come to you in the heart of the compass to ask direction."

"Where do you wish to journey?"

"To a place called London."

"When do you wish to visit?"

"The present, Mother."

"All for the Good, Daughter."

"For the Good of All, Mother."

Rose looked up as the roof dissolved. She'd seen the universe revealed hundreds of times before, but she couldn't help purring at each unveiling. Many galaxies filled the sky, and Rose recognized the stars closest to Earth as glowing gemstones: emeralds, rubies, sapphires and tiger's eye. Silver threads connected the stars, forming a vast net. Rose took a deep breath, until part of the gleaming net began to pulse inside her. The way to London had become a part of her.

"Thank you, Mother."

"Safe journey, Daughter."

Rose stepped into the star map. If all went well, she'd soon find Nick's father, Byron.

Fight

Early the next morning, Nick stalked into the garden, ignoring the snow underfoot. He wanted lots of distance between him and Rose.

"I was a fool!" he ranted inside. "If she can't even deliver a simple message, there's no way she can get me to my other lives. How could I be so stupid?" He'd trusted Rose and made himself vulnerable. And now he had only dashed hopes to show for it. Nick paced back and forth, his tail swiping from side to side. On his next turn toward the house he found Rose crouched two feet from him, barring his path.

"Nick, I'm sorry I couldn't deliver your message."

"I thought you knew what you were doing," Nick hissed at her.

Rose recoiled from Nick's words as if he'd physically swiped at her. But her firm voice told him she had not accepted his rebuke.

"I know you did, and I promise to try again. But I'll have to search for your father elsewhere. The Guardian of the Tower Ravens is a white shorthair by the name of Athos."

"No. You went to the wrong place. My father's name is Byron, and he's a tabby."

"I found the Tower of London, Nick. Your dad resigned nearly two years ago, and now Athos and his family live there. He didn't know why your father left, but he hasn't seen him since and doesn't know anyone who has."

"And I'm telling you that my father would never leave the Ravens or the Tower. He loved his wo—"

At the sound of the kitchen door, both feline heads swiveled in the direction of the house. Bart left the back porch for the garden and crossed to the stone bench, clearing a place to sit beneath the leafless elm tree. He plunked down with his typical lack of grace, never taking his eyes from Nick and Rose.

"Well, what have we here, a spat between fleabags?" Bart asked in a sneering tone. "Looks like you're on the outs, blue boy. Glad to see you've finally worn out your welcome with the spoiled princess." Bart's smug smile revealed yellow, picket teeth.

Neither Rose nor Nick moved. The two felines watched Bart, and Nick knew Rose wanted the man to go away as much as he did. Bart pointed a thick index finger at Nick, emphasizing each word.

"You. Make. Me. Puke. Adele wastes enough time on the other two. So you can go right back to the hole you slunk out of."

Nick stood his ground watching Bart, his tail moving in angry rhythm.

"You heard me. Go on, get outta here!" Bart grabbed the metal watering can from the bench and pulled back to hurl it at Nick, water and all. But in the instant before his arm swung forward, Rose leaped at Bart, claws out. She landed on Bart's leg just above the ankle, and from his cry of shock and pain, Nick knew she'd dug in with her teeth too.

As Bart dropped the watering can and reached to grab Rose, Nick reacted without hesitation. He ran toward the screaming human and infuriated feline, jumped to the bench and sunk his own teeth and claws into Bart's forearm.

Bart yelled even louder in a roar of fury. Nick's grip prevented Bart from reaching Rose, but she cried out as Bart shook his leg loose of her hold. His kick sent her a foot into the air and nearly across the garden.

"Stop! Bart, stop! What are you doing?" Adele screamed. She pushed through the backdoor, crossed the yard, and grabbed Nick around his belly. "Let go, Blue, it's okay, let go now."

At Adele's urging, Nick released his hold on Bart. Smoke came around the corner and ran through the snow to Rose. Adele followed, still clutching Nick to her. She put Nick down and sank to her knees beside Rose.

Rose lay panting, her belly pressed to the ground. She licked Adele's hand, but Nick could see she was in pain.

Adele could see it too. She explored Rose's body with gentle hands. "No broken bones," she said aloud. Then she stood up and stalked back to Bart with long strides.

"What happened?" she asked her husband between lips tight with anger.

"You saw 'em! Your precious cats attacked me, two against one. Came at me out of nowhere. They're probably rabid!"

Adele said nothing, but her hands were clenched into fists at her side.

"Here I am bleeding, covered with scratches and bites an' you're worried about THEM!" Bart stamped both feet and pointed a shaking fist at the cats.

Adele stood her ground. "I saw you kick Rose across the yard, an animal a tenth your size! And I know she would never attack you unless—if she's badly hurt, I'll…"

Bart's eyes went stone cold. "You'll what, Adele?"

Adele took a deep breath, but she did not step back. "Go inside. I'll be in to put something on your scratches."

"Just don't make me wait too long." Bart looked over at the cats and spat. He opened the kitchen door and stalked inside.

Adele turned to the three tense cats watching from the fence line. Rose stood to walk toward Adele, limping on her left rear leg. Adele bent down and gently cradled Rose in her arms. "I'm so, so sorry," she whispered into Rose's fur, tears bright on her face. "I'm so sorry."

The woman took a moment to collect herself, wiping tears from her cheeks with the back of one hand. She carried Rose through the back garden around the cottage and onto the front porch. Nick and Smoke followed. They watched Adele remove her sweater to create a soft bed for Rose on the white wicker chair.

"You alright?" Smoke asked Nick.

"I'm fine," Nick answered, "but I don't care how cold it gets tonight, I'm not going in there."

"Understood. I'll sit with Rose until Bart goes to bed. Then I'll come find you. I want to hear what really happened."

Once Smoke took up position beside Rose, Adele entered the

house.

Nick stretched to release built up tension, and then moved off in the direction of the tool shed. From there, he could hear Bart's squawks and rants as Adele cleaned his wounds. But what Nick really wanted was a good view of the house. He'd know if Bart went anywhere near Rose and Smoke.

Adele Departs

Two weeks later, the cats' daily routines were back to normal, but life had changed: Rose remained stiff and slow moving, and Nick noticed that Adele encouraged her to stay close by. That meant Smoke, his sister's faithful bodyguard, also shadowed Adele. And Nick had begun to track Bart's every movement whenever he and the man were both in the house.

Coming in from the cold garden that morning, Nick sauntered into the kitchen, and headed for the water bowl. His thirst satisfied, he followed his nose to Rose and Smoke and found the siblings seated side-by-side near the front door of the cottage.

They were watching Adele tie a winter scarf around her neck. A small brown valise sat at the woman's feet, and she reached for her winter coat. Nick could feel stress rolling off his friends.

"What's up?" Nick asked.

"Adele is leaving to visit her mother in the city," Rose answered. Rose was agitated, but working hard to appear calm. "Will she be back by dinner time?" asked Nick.

Smoke shook his head, his expression grim.

"Bart, I've left plenty of food for you and cooked chicken for the cats. You won't forget to feed them will you?" Adele called.

Bart grunted from his chair in the parlor.

Now Nick was worried. Adele would be gone long enough that she'd made food in advance, and they'd be dependent on Bart for meals at home.

"Do you want to walk me to the station?" Adele asked Bart.

When Bart didn't respond, Adele took a deep breath, stepped into the small room and crossed to her husband's chair at the fireside. "Please don't be angry. It's not my fault Mother has hurt her hip too badly to care for herself."

Bart continued to slump unmoving in his chair, his brooding glare pinned to the thick flames in the grate.

"She needs me. You can see that, can't you?"

"Why did she have to fall so close to Christmas?" Bart sulked. "Who's gonna make the pies and treats?"

The cats saw Adele grit her teeth, but she answered in a cheery voice. "With luck, Mother will be up and around in a week. Christmas is still two weeks away, so I should be home in plenty of time."

"Well, you better be."

Adele leaned down, left a glancing kiss on Bart's cheek and returned to her valise. Instead of reaching for the handle, she crouched down and took Rose into her arms.

"I'll look for you in my dreams, little love," she whispered looking into Rose's green eyes. "And you stick close to Smoke and Blue. They'll watch out for you."

Next, Adele hoisted Smoke to her shoulder, held him close and scratched beneath his chin. Smoke didn't usually like to be picked up, but he purred, nestled in the woman's arms.

"You take care of the others, Smoke. I know you'll do that for me."

Smoke licked Adele's nose in confirmation.

Adele returned Smoke to the floor, and reached toward Nick, but she did not try to pick him up. Instead, she stroked his ear and ran her hand down his furry, blue back.

"You stay out of trouble, my friend. And help Smoke protect Rose."

Nick rubbed his cheek against her outstretched hand. Adele smiled in acknowledgement and stood up. Nick could feel her reluctance to leave.

"Goodbye, then, Bart," she called. "Please take good care of yourself and the cats. I'll be back as soon as I can."

Adele paused long enough for Bart to answer, but when he didn't, she stepped through the door and closed it behind her. All three cats rushed to the parlor windowseat. They watched Adele walk through the snow in the garden. As she closed the garden gate behind her, she turned and looked back. Her smile was wistful as she waved a mittened hand in farewell.

Then she walked down the street, turned the corner, and was gone. Smoke gave a silent meow of goodbye. Rose sighed. And Nick felt the house shrink and grow darker.

Sean Leaves

Sean glanced at the wall calendar: December 11th. Mark had left for school, but Minette sat across from him, still wrapped in her cozy nightgown and thick robe. For several heartbeats, Sean watched Minette look from the red thread in her right hand, to the needle in her left. Finally, he gently took both from her, threaded the needle, tied a knot in the end of the double loop and handed them back. Minette's face lit with delighted surprise, and nodding her thanks, she bent to her stitching.

But Sean couldn't share his wife's happiness. Her memory loss grew worse each week. He was losing his best friend, and he could do nothing about it. He groaned with helpless frustration.

Minette looked up. "Are you alright? Did you prick your finger?"

"No, Love, I'm fine. It's nothing." Sean turned away before Minette could see his despair. He stood, picked up the note he'd written and went upstairs to Mark's loft. He came back downstairs, tugged on his winter boots, shoved into his coat and pulled his blue muffler from the wooden peg by the door. He crossed the room and knelt to look into his wife's face. "I love you, Minette," he said.

"And I love you," Minette answered with a loving smile.

For a moment, Sean could believe that all the months of loss were just a bad dream.

"Have you seen, Mira?" Minette asked. "I must feed her soon."

Sean's hopes shattered. Mira had been Minette's dog, but her beloved pet had died over twenty years ago. His wife's mind was wandering in the past again.

Sean leaned forward, kissed Minette and rose to his feet. He didn't look back as he pulled the carved door closed behind him.

Chapter Nineteen

Captive Cats

With Adele gone, Bart abandoned all normal hours and responsibilities. He drank into the night, and broke into screaming fits without any warning or provocation. The cottage soon smelled of unwashed human and cloying alcohol.

"Sure, I'll just waste my time watching over the fleabags," Bart ranted. "Well, we'll just see about that. Come on, you rotten parasites, I dare you to take what's coming to you."

The cats' nerves were soon frayed, and though they hated to give up the warmth of the parlor fire, the three friends melted from the room until Bart's grinding snores signaled they could come out of hiding. Finding food became a daily chore, and deep snow on the ground slowed hunting. Nick and Smoke's pact didn't help either: If Bart was in the house with Rose, either Nick or Smoke remained home too. Rose would never have agreed, but that's why they kept their plan a secret.

"I can't believe Adele's not back yet," Smoke said, his eyes locked to the garden gate. If staring at the spot could make the woman reappear, she'd have been home the same day she left.

"Feels like months," Nick agreed. They both knew that the sun had risen and set seven times since then.

"I hope she comes back today," said Smoke, "but she's not going to like what she finds whenever she gets here."

Nick just nodded. Even he knew Adele would be upset when she saw the state of her husband, her home and her beloved cats.

And the next morning, Bart must have imagined Adele's reaction too. He muttered in low, angry tones, as he paced through the cottage rooms, a simmering storm of discontent. Outside, snow had been falling hard and heavy since dawn. It was Nick's turn to hunt, but he'd delayed going out into the cold as long as possible.

It was mid-morning when he finally arrived back at the cottage tired and cold, but successful. He'd had breakfast, and then caught a large mouse for Rose and Smoke to share. He took the route through the cellar, and climbed up through the cats' entry hole beside the laundry tub.

He dropped the mouse on the wooden floor and went in search of his friends. He stepped through the silent kitchen and headed for the parlor, but found no one. Nick padded down the short hall, and paused at the door to the bedroom. Bart's smell hung heavy in the room, and Nick expected to see him facedown drooling atop the bedcovers. But the man wasn't in sight, and neither were Smoke and Rose.

Nick prickled with unease. He spun around to head back to the exit hole, just as a net, reeking of salt and dead fish dropped over him. Nick was stunned still for an instant, then he was biting and clawing at the thick threads with all his strength.

"Now who's special?" Bart bleated. He gathered up the net until Nick hung in midair and upside down. Bart's face gloated just out of claw reach. Holding the net in one hand, he crossed the room, and opened the closet door. Nick's heart sank. He could hear Smoke and Rose's frightened cries as Bart tossed aside the comforters and pillows piled atop a burlap sack on the closet floor.

Nick struggled with all his strength to break free, but Bart grabbed him by the back of the neck and tossed him into the sack. Nick landed on his back, crushed against Rose. Smoke was on the bottom of the pile. Nick couldn't see his friends' faces, but he could smell their fear, and his own mouth filled with the bitter taste of panic. He felt as stupid as a newborn kitten for letting his guard down around Bart. He could hear the man's laughter, dripping with malice.

Nick panted to regain the breath knocked out of him. He strained to turn over without injuring Rose, as Bart tied a rope around the sack opening, and cinched it tight. The bag jerked up and off the floor. They were moving.

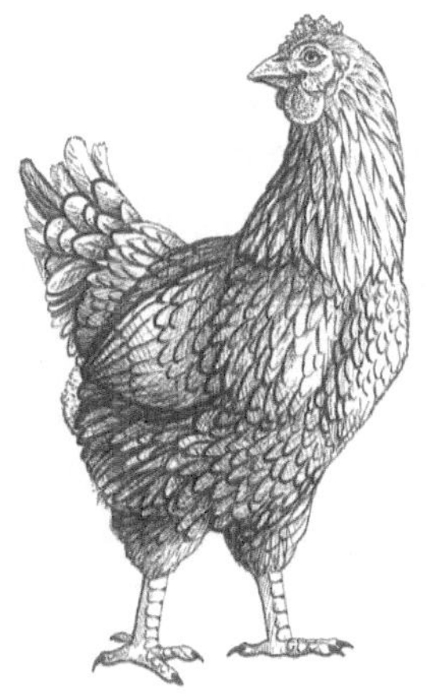

Betrayed

This is it," Bart announced, jerking the wooden wagon to a stop. He'd driven for most of the day, and he'd be returning in the dark. But this desolate spot was worth the effort. "This will be jusssssst perfect."

He sat savoring the sting of the wind and the bleak isolation of the mountain crossroad, his eyes grey flint beneath a greasy hat. With a chuckle, he reached back, grabbed the squirming bag, and dangled it at eye level over the wagon's edge. "Now let's see you try to steal food from my mouth!" he bellowed.

The squirming stopped.

Bart leaned close to the burlap sack as if to whisper a secret. "And when Adele asks me where you are, I'll look her right in the eye and say, 'I have no idea, sweetheart'."

He opened his meaty fist, and the bundle smacked into the snow. His lips twisted into a smile at the muffled cries of pain. He spat over the wagon-side, splattering the sack with sticky tobacco juice.

"Take that too." With a final grunt of satisfaction, Bart slashed his whip across the hip of his neighbor's scrawny mule. Straining, she pulled the wagon around and headed toward home.

Nick finally broke through the sack and stepped out on cautious paws, ears straining for sounds of danger. He saw only jagged peaks covered in snow and a few scattered trees in the distance. Bart had dropped them at the bleak intersection of two mountain roads. Bart and the cart were long gone, the wheel ruts filling in with drifting snow.

Rose crawled out behind Nick. Despite her thick coat, she shivered.

"I don't care what's out there, it's gotta be better than this stinking sack," said Smoke's muffled voice.

"I wouldn't be so sure," Rose warned.

Smoke dragged himself free, and took in the barren terrain. He snorted in wordless agreement. "Right. So let's huddle and come up with a plan."

A heartbeat later, the three friends crouched in a tight circle, back to back, eyes scanning the horizon. No one needed to point out that their situation was dire, starting with the bitter cold and ending with the absence of food and shelter.

"If we get going, we could still end up home beside the warm fire on Christmas morning," urged Rose.

"'Home?'" Nick exploded. "We're days of walking from 'home.' And right now the only one there is the guy who brought us out here to die. Bart will just try to kill us again—only quicker next time."

"Agreed," said Smoke.

At that moment, the wind gusted, buffeting the cats with frigid snow. They closed their eyes, crouched closer together and waited for the flurry to die down.

"But we have to head somewhere," Smoke continued, looking up. "Those clouds are coming in fast, and they're loaded with more snow."

Rose nodded in grim confirmation. "But which way?" she asked. "I don't smell anything remotely like food, shelter, or ho…" she trailed off.

Rose and Smoke looked over their shoulders at Nick. But Nick hadn't heard the question, or noticed his friends' expectant stares. He was too consumed with disappointment and rage. The best months of his life were over, and there was only one person to blame. Nick made a silent promise to himself: If he ever saw Bart again, he'd shred him until he bled from head to foot, and was blind to boot.

"Nick…?" Rose prompted.

Still lost in visions of a bloody Bart, Nick heard Rose's voice from far away. He brought her face into focus.

"Which way do you think we should go?" she asked.

Nick returned his gaze to the wasteland of white. He'd decided which way to go moments after he'd escaped the sack. "I'm going that way." Nick tilted his head toward the road on his right winding steeply down out of sight below them.

"Okay, we'd better get started then," said Smoke rising from his crouch.

Rose stood up beside him, preparing to move, fluffing her neck fur for warmth. But Nick remained crouched, staring straight ahead. "You two don't get it, do you?" he said.

Rose huddled closer to Smoke. "We know that we're in grave danger," she said in a careful voice, "and that you're our best chance to survive."

Nick snorted. "Our chances of surviving are nonexistent. If we're very lucky, and if we manage to cover lots of ground at top speed, one—at most two of us—may live."

Smoke drilled angry eyes into Nick. "That's enough, Nick. We'll just have to do the best we can," he growled, his hackles rising.

Nick stood up, his eyes flaming. "This is it for me! If you guys die in this life, you'll still pop up in one of your other eight. But this is the only life I have. I've got to move fast and fend for myself. I've got to survive." Nick looked away. He knew he was right. But he clamped his jaws to choke down his shame.

The siblings were silent. After several heartbeats, Nick saw Rose look at Smoke, and Nick knew a decision had passed between the two cats. Rose turned back to Nick, and Smoke looked down, focusing on the snow at his feet.

"You're wrong, Nick. We don't both have eight lives waiting for us."

"What? Is this some kind of—?"

"This is Smoke's last life," Rose said in a firm voice. "All of his other lives have ended. Just like you, he has only this one."

Nick's jaw dropped, but he could see Rose was telling the truth. He turned to Smoke, who looked back at him with quiet dignity. So much suddenly made sense—Smoke's reluctance to discuss his other lives, this life being his "favorite," and the devotion between sister and brother. Nick was hit with sorrow for his friend. He knew exactly how it felt to have only one, short life. He always had.

But their chances of survival were dropping every moment they sat still.

Nick reached a decision. "I can't promise I'll slow down if either of you falter, but we've got to go now." He wheeled around and headed down the hillside at the fastest pace he could manage in the deep snow. Rose and Smoke set off after him.

CHAPTER TWENTY-ONE

A Beastly Boogle

Many snow-covered miles away, in a den deep beneath the roots of the forest, another confrontation was taking place.

"Medusa, if you bump my tail one more time, you'll have one less thing to worry about—your future!" snarled Rogo. He was a big-muscled, brown weasel, and picking fights was his favorite pastime. Rogo had two habits that put his fun in easy reach: He always insisted on getting his way. And, whether they were interested or not, he constantly pointed out the many faults and flaws he found with the entire boogle of weasels.

They had reveled through the sunny months of spring and

summer. They'd eaten until their stomachs ached without the slightest thought of the lean winter months ahead, thanks to one of Rogo's pet phrases: "Tomorrow is somebody else's problem." Any weasel who tried to hide winter rations from Rogo and his bullies was soon driven out to the tune of Rogo's favorite taunt: "Less is for Losers." But now in the depths of cold December, discontent and hunger fueled foul moods.

"This den is a dump," Rogo growled, "and there's nothin' good left to eat. I oughta get myself outta here and leave the rest of you to starve."

It was easy to see why anyone would want to leave this weasel den for somewhere, or anywhere, else. A stench of decay hung nearly visible in the air. Rotted apple cores, the shattered shells of pilfered nuts and eggs, and a bleak collection of gnawed bones littered the floor. Former food and other unmentionables lay in ripe puddles throughout the underground nest.

As he cast a surly eye over den and denizens alike, a plan hatched in Rogo's brain—a plan both unpleasant and mean-spirited. And that suited the gnarly brown weasel just fine.

"Listen you miserable excuses for weasels. Right over that hill Dreamhaven village is crawling with Christmas goodies," Rogo wheedled in a mocking voice. "Hah! My dreams would be great too if I had a full stomach. The village is ripe for the picking. Why shouldn't we feast this Christmas?" Rogo ranted.

Not one of the two-dozen reeking weasels could think of a reason why not. Rogo paced with pleasure, fueled by the promise of action and stolen food. But he didn't mention the real prize he sought in Dreamhaven. Not yet. Once the boogle ran loose in the village, there'd be plenty of opportunities for Rogo to take his revenge.

Snickering with anticipation, he came up with a new slogan,

and soon the den rang with raucous weasel voices. "Christmas comes but once a year! Rip it! Wreck it! Christmas Cheer!"

As night fell, Rogo repeated his instructions. "...so remember, our strength is in numbers. Everyone follows me. Where I go, you go. By the time we're done with Dreamhaven, they'll rename it 'Nightmare Village'."

That night, twenty-five hungry weasels emptied out of the den, a dark wave of wicked intentions streaming across the white snow, headed straight for Dreamhaven.

CHAPTER TWENTY-TWO

Abandoned

As the other children bundled up and left the schoolroom, Mr. Wolfram returned Mark's arithmetic test. "I couldn't help but notice the unusual number of errors in your test, Mark. We could go over them now, if you like," he said in a quiet voice.

Mark's face flushed with embarrassment. "Sorry, Mr. Wolfram. I can't stay today. But I'll do better next time." He hadn't been able to concentrate during the test—or all week. He jammed his test and books into his rucksack and stumbled toward the schoolroom door.

"Is everything all right? Are you ill?" Mr. Wolfram asked.

With a dread he'd never felt before, Mark turned to face the man now leaning against the edge of his massive pine desk.

"I only ask because these quiz problems wouldn't normally stump you. And you seem tired."

Mark really liked Mr. Wolfram. He kept lessons interesting and generously lent Mark fantastic books by Robert Louis Stevenson and Mr. Verne. But now Mark felt cornered. He stared at the wool mitten his mother had knitted for him last Christmas. So far, only Mark and his father knew how fast his mother's mind was slipping away. And though father and son had never said so aloud, Mark knew that for now, neither of them felt ready to talk about it with anyone else. He raised his eyes to Mr. Wolfram's face. "I'm fine, Mr. Wolfram. I'm just…excited about Christmas. It's pretty close now."

Mr. Wolfram said nothing, but his solemn gaze remained focused on Mark's face. Mark returned to studying the intricate pattern of his mitten. Finally, Mr. Wolfram spoke. "Yes, of course you're excited. Father Christmas will reach Dreamhaven soon. I'll see you tomorrow."

·§·

Mark stood at his cottage door, shivering in the icy breeze. He'd hurried home, but now that he'd arrived, he didn't really want to raise the latch and go inside. Would his mother welcome him home and ask about his day? Those days were fewer and fewer. And where was his father?

Ten days ago Mark had come home from school to find his mother still in her nightgown, and a short note in his father's broad handwriting atop his pillow.

Mark, I've gone to find a dog for your mother. It's the only Christmas present I can think of. Maybe having a dog like Mira will help her—or at least make her happy. There's plenty of wood and smoked meat, and I've chosen a Christmas tree for the house. It's on the west side. You'll see my red bandana. Don't skip school. Your mother will have my hide if you do. Be a good boy, son.

Your Dad

Remembering his father's note, Mark exhaled a slow breath, but his lips clenched tight. For the last ten mornings, Mark had left for school worried about leaving his mother alone in the house. From the moment school started to the minute it let out, he felt anxious. Yesterday he hadn't been able to stand the suspense. He'd mumbled some excuse and raced home to check on her.

Each day, Mark had expected to open the cottage door and see his father sitting in his chair by the fire. But today, just like all ten days before, Mark alone would face whatever problems waited on the other side of the door. He closed his eyes, inhaled deeply and stepped over the threshold.

"Mom, I'm home."

His mother sat at on a bench at the kitchen table. She looked up with a surprised smile.

"Mark? Why did you go to school on a Saturday?" she asked.

Mark guessed she'd been staring at her hands or her sewing machine, trying to remember what to do with them. Her confusion made him sad, but today she seemed okay otherwise. Mark kissed her cheek.

"Today's Thursday, Mom. I'll get us some wood."

At nightfall, though he moved like a sleepwalker, Mark continued his chores, building fires in the grate and stove, and putting together an early dinner for two as best he could. He encouraged his mother to eat. Between bites she asked him questions he couldn't answer.

"Where is Mira? Why is your father so late tonight? Do you

think he'll get home in time to decorate the tree?"

"Don't worry, Mom. Dad'll be here soon," Mark answered with false confidence. Against his will, he looked over at the fir tree standing bare in the corner of the room. Three days ago he'd finally cut down the eight–foot beauty his father had selected for their Christmas tree. Then he'd loaded the tree on the sled, and with many grunts, pulled it to the cottage. With his mother's help, he'd managed to get the tree inside and upright. But he hadn't been able to bring himself to begin decorating its branches.

"Only four days left to Christmas," Minette said, pointing to the wall calendar. "Why isn't your Dad here to decorate the tree with us?"

Every Christmas Mark and his parents had laughed together and pretended to argue over which of them would hang the prettiest ornaments. If his dad were coming back, wouldn't he be here by now? Mark clenched his mug in both hands, ignoring the burn in his palms from the heated cider. There. He'd said it—at least to himself: *If* his father was coming home.

Mark looked at his mother. How could he miss her so much, when she sat right here? She was repeating the same ritual of the previous three nights. She pulled back the cotton wrappings and removed a glass ornament from the special wooden box his father had made. She held the fragile globe up to the light and smiled. Then she returned that one to its place and selected another.

Mark had never felt so alone. His chin dropped to his chest. He sat, too tired to move, the wooden cuckoo clock ticking away the minutes. The next time Mark looked up, he'd made two decisions. The first, he would take care of right now. The other he'd put into action later that night—if he could make himself.

"Come on, Mom, let's decorate the tree," he said aloud.

CHAPTER TWENTY-THREE

A Slippery Slope

Nick! Nick, wait!" Smoke called again.

Against his will, Nick stopped, turned, and sat down in the snow-covered road. He watched the grey cat's determined stride through lengthening shadows. It was late afternoon and they'd been on the move without stopping since morning. They had little progress to show for their three days homeless.

The day Bart dumped them, Nick had set a fast pace until sundown. That night, he'd found an abandoned fox den and bedded down. Rose and Smoke had eventually arrived and fallen asleep beside him. They'd lost any chance to travel the second day, trapped in the fox den by a new storm. As he waited for Smoke to catch up, Nick sniffed the air for scents of prey, food or wood fire. Nothing. The third day would slip into cold evening too soon.

He'd had nothing to eat since his breakfast at Bart's two mornings before. Smoke and Rose hadn't even gotten that meal, and Nick could see that Smoke was definitely worse for wear. He moved on stiff muscles, his face stretched with fatigue. Nick understood Smoke's pain from the sting of his own, and he knew he looked as bad as, if not worse, than Smoke.

"Nick, you…" Smoke stopped to breathe. He started again. "Nick, you've got to slow down. Rose and I can't keep up."

Nick looked up at the brooding sky. He kept his gaze there instead of looking into his friend's eyes. "I can't do that, Smoke. My…our only chance is finding shelter and food before the next storm hits." Nick looked directly at Smoke. "You know that as well as I do."

Smoke's chest heaved from his run, but the rest of his muscles went still. He looked down at the snow. Nick assumed the whole truth had just hit Smoke, and the grey cat didn't want Nick to see his fear.

"I'm more sorry than I can say. The truth is, Rose has already given up, but you—"

Smoke's head snapped up. The anger in his eyes hit Nick like a kick. "She hasn't given up! She's still injured from attacking Bart to defend you!" Smoke hissed. "If I hadn't brought you home, she wouldn't be out here at all. You were one cat too many."

Nick's empty stomach tightened in a knot. He dropped his head, unable to look Smoke in the eyes. He hadn't felt this way since he'd seen London slipping away from him.

"And she's lost Adele too, so don't you ever call her a quitter."

Now Nick's eyes flashed. "She's dragging her belly over a human? A human tossed us out here to die!" he spat.

"I know that, and so does Rose. But that was Bart, not Adele, and you know it. She loved us—including you."

Both cats fell silent under the weight of loss. Smoke spoke first. "Rose has been using her energy to try to reach Adele in dream to ask for her help."

Surprise took the edge off Nick's anger. "Rose can share dreams with humans too?" The possibility of bonding that closely with a human had never entered his mind.

"Rose and Adele have shared dreams for years."

Nick remembered Adele's parting words to Rose: "I'll look for you in my dreams." He hadn't understood then. But it didn't matter now. He couldn't count on Rose or Adele. He stood up.

"I'm sorry, Smoke."

Smoke's voice became a low growl. "When I first saw you passed out in that alley, I felt sorry for you. I could smell the fear and blood on you. But all the trouble you'd passed through worked like catnip on me. I thought you could teach me courage."

"Smoke, I—"

Smoke cut him off. "But I was a fool. You don't know anything about courage—or loyalty."

Smoke rose and shook his trembling body once. Then he turned away from Nick and loped back the way he'd come, doing his best to make fast time despite his failing strength.

Nick watched until Smoke disappeared around a curve in the road. He hung his head, stunned by Smoke's words and the sight of his friend's retreating tracks.

But going back meant death. Before he could change his mind, Nick spun around and resumed his pace in the opposite direction. As he walked on, Nick struggled with more than freezing paws and the growing temptation to lie down for a nap. He knew sleep was deadly. He forced himself to focus on his next step. But nothing could stop him from remembering the despair in Smoke's eyes, or from hearing the bitter echo of his friend's accusations.

What if Smoke was right? What if he was the reason Bart had snapped and dumped them out here? Nick felt certain the man had always meant trouble for the siblings, but he hadn't made his move until Nick came along. Maybe Rose wouldn't have attacked Bart if Nick hadn't berated her for not delivering his message.

Nick walked on, his pace slowing with the weight of his thoughts. Smoke had given him more than food and shelter. The grey cat had welcomed him into his home, and Smoke and Rose had become Nick's first—and only friends.

Nick looked up at the sound of a bird in flight. A young owl flew over him, the body of a long-tailed mouse clamped in its beak. Nick's empty stomach cramped, his whiskers twitched and he dropped to a crouch.

The bird, no larger than Nick, swooped low to the ground, and then out of sight over a hill to the right of the road. Nick didn't want to climb that rise, but if the bird had landed, maybe he could sneak up on him. Even if the bird got away, he might have to leave that carcass behind. That mouse was the first sign of food in two days.

Still hugging the snow, Nick left the road and padded up the hill, hoping the growl of his stomach wouldn't alert his prey. Despite his fear of lethal talons, every inch of Nick ached to catch that bird. But as he paused and flattened himself even lower to peer over the hilltop, the owl rose straight into the air, taking his meal with him.

Nick was disgusted. The climb had been a waste of energy, and now he was even hungrier than before. He turned to retrace his steps down the hill, pausing to look back for Rose and Smoke.

The snow beneath his feet shuddered. Nick tried to push off the collapsing powder to solid footing. But he was too late.

The Decision

"Did you see that?" Rose asked. "Nick was up on that high snow bank—and then he was gone."

"What else is new?" Smoke didn't lift his eyes from the track in front of him. That would take energy he didn't have.

"No, this was different. He was facing us, and then he just… vanished. I don't think even Nick could move that fast."

"And I think he's done a brilliant job of disappearing for three days." Smoke didn't bother to disguise his bitterness.

"Fine. But I'm going to head in that direction to be sure he isn't in some kind of trouble."

Smoke's laugh edged on hysteria. "'In some kind of trouble?' What worse trouble could he possibly be in?"

But Rose was already on the move. Against his better judgment, Smoke followed, if only because he felt too tired to argue. Fifteen minutes later brother and sister intersected Nick's paw prints and followed them off the road. Before they'd reached the top of the hill, Smoke froze in his tracks.

"Rose, stop! The snow's unstable," he warned.

"Nick? Nick, where are you?" Rose called. Despite Smoke's warning, she continued up the hill to the top.

"Save your breath. Nick's sprinted ahead, or found a cave, or…he's gone." Smoke reversed direction to return the way they'd come. "So let's just get back to the road and keep—"

"I found him. He's down there."

His concern for the soft snow forgotten, Smoke stood beside his sister in an instant. He followed her gaze over and down the sharp edge. He saw churned snow piled in a gully below them. A collapsed snow bridge. A dozen feet below their perch, Nick lay in a mess of snow and boulders. He wasn't moving.

"Hisssssssss." Smoke exhaled his horror.

"Nick, we're coming right now," Rose called, in a voice that belied the fear coiled in her belly. Nick didn't respond.

"No we're not." Smoke blocked her way as she moved to go back and down around the rock pile. "We're getting back on that road now. There's nothing we can do for Nick."

Rose looked into her brother's molten eyes. "You don't know that. We have to get to him."

Smoke remained unmoving. "He's unconscious, and probably hurt beyond anything we can do. If he's broken a leg, letting him—sleep—is best.

"We don't know that he's broken anything."

"But we do know that we need every bit of energy we've got." Smoke's eyes held a mix of sadness and steel. "And we don't have any to spare for climbing down there and back up to the road." Smoke's eyes held a mix of sadness and steel. "It's what he'd do if we were lying down there, Rose."

Rose absorbed Smoke's words, and then dropped to a crouch. She took a deep breath. Smoke was right about their fading energy. The jolts that had zinged through her at the first sight of Nick were ebbing away, leaving behind even deeper exhaustion. She should try to use her gift first, but…Rose couldn't stop a shiver that had nothing to do with the cold. Though she'd offered to help Nick, she'd seen what his dreams did to him: The cries in his sleep, the horror and pain in his eyes when he first awoke from them. Maybe Nick's dreams were dangerous to him and to her too. But at least in dream, they were no threat to Smoke. Rose swallowed her panic and closed her eyes. A silent minute ticked by.

When she returned, her voice was soft and urgent. "I love you, Smoke. I know you're trying to protect and care for me, and everything you say may be true. But I can't go on without knowing if we could have—"

Smoke cut her off. "Did you try to reach Nick in dream?"

"Yes, but it's not working. All I see in Nick's current dream is black. I guess, I'm too tired or too weak or…I don't know why it's failing."

"Maybe you can't reach him because he's damaged beyond repair. Or dead."

"I don't know what the blackness means. Nick isn't like any dreamer I've ever met. Maybe I just need to get closer…" Rose's voice trailed off into a whisper. "But if I leave now, and we somehow survive, I'll always wonder. And that would be like leaving a part of myself here to die with Nick."

Rose stood up. "You don't have to come with me, but I'm going down there."

"Splitting up is the worst thing we could do." Smoke's words were a plea. But he could see that Rose's decision was final.

"Then I'll lead," he said. He moved past her, his voice drifting back over his shoulder. "If it were just Nick and I, I'd already be down there."

"I know."

Once committed, both cats wanted to race to Nick's side. But picking their way around boulders and over snow bridges proved slow going. Ten minutes later, the siblings crouched beside Nick.

"Well, he's breathing, and…I don't see any sign of injury." Smoke found himself whispering. "But we don't know what's happening on the inside."

Rose stepped closer to Nick, and spoke into his ear, "Nick, wake up. We're here. It's Rose and Smoke."

Nick didn't even twitch.

Rose looked at Smoke across Nick's still body. "I'm going to find out what I can in dream."

Smoke nodded, his stomach a tight knot. He would be their only protection against predators. And he could not help Rose face Nick's dream.

"I love you, Smoke." Rose bumped against her beloved brother, and then nestled up to Nick, her spine against his. She closed her eyes and slipped into dream.

CHAPTER TWENTY-FIVE

Flying Alli

Mark's right foot slipped out from under him, then his left. For a few moments he dangled by his hands, but his precarious grip on the smooth outcropping above him wouldn't last. He groaned, accepting the inevitable: The pulsing crystal mountain had beaten him again. He hit the orange snow and rolled several times, barely missing the pine tree, to land at Shift's armored feet.

Shift shook his current head, a wombat, in tepid sympathy, as he waited for Mark to sit up. "Are you willing to admit we need some help?" He asked. That's the third time you've fallen."

"Fourth. The fourth time," Mark croaked still trying to catch his breath.

"I was being kind. My point is, at this rate, they'll move the treasure long before we reach the top. We need to get up there soon."

"Okay, but how? We can't fly, and short of that, I don't see— why are you looking at me like that?"

Shift's wombat eyes glittered with excitement. "We don't need to fly! Not if we catch a ride on…"

"Alli!" Mark and Shift yelled in unison.

"Shift, you're brilliant. Call him. With Alli, we'll have that gold in a flash."

Shift nodded. "I'll try. But you know how he is. If he's got something better to do, he won't show." Shift raised his head to sing a series of clicks and hoots that rose and fell in a surreal melody. He'd repeated the song twice, when a twelve-foot long shadow formed against the purple sky above them.

"You did it. He's here!"

The alligator floated like a balloon, but his sinister grin squashed any thoughts of children's parties. Unlike his earth-bound cousins, Alli's feet were webbed to help him steer as he flew through the air. The creature tilted to the left, dropping a thick rope beside Mark and Shift. Mark pulled down hard, tug-ging their ride closer in a steady descent.

Thanks for coming, Alli," Mark said when the unblinking behemoth, hovered a foot above the snow. Alli opened his mas-sive jaws once in recognition, and waited as Mark re-coiled the rope, looped it around the alligator's left leg, and set Shift atop his back. Mark took his seat behind Shift, and grabbed the rope in both hands. When Mark nodded to show he was ready, Alli shoved with powerful legs and swam upward in a vertical climb. Mark and Shift leaned forward to keep their seats. They were laughing, urging Alli on, when Mark heard his name.

"Mark? It's time to get up," his mother called.

Mark groaned, and lay with his eyes closed for a long minute. Then he threw off the comforter with both arms and shuffled to the table in the corner. He added some water from the ewer, grabbed a slab of village-made soap and started scrubbing. He worked fast, urged on by his goose bumps. By the time he'd dried and hung the towel on its peg, every muscle was reminding him how far he'd hauled the Christmas tree. He flexed his long fingers. His hands were sore from pulling on the rope. Then he remembered gripping the other rope as Alli swam for the sky. Smiling, he headed downstairs.

He was outside gathering wood when his mother called to him from the back door.

"Mark, there's someone here to see you."

He looked up and caught her smile before she turned away. She was having a good day. And his father was finally home. He rushed inside to find five-year-old Nathan sitting at the kitchen table.

"Nathan? What are you doing here?" Mark blurted, too surprised to hide his disappointment.

"Tutoring, remember?"

"Yeah, but I come to you, remember?" Mark answered, mimicking Nathan's know-it-all tone. He'd changed his arrangement with Nathan's grandmother since the start of Fall term. He hadn't wanted Nathan to see his mom's condition, or have him confuse her with his constant questions.

"Your mom makes better cookies. 'Sides, you said I could help you with Clavier's Beacon this week."

"But you shouldn't—"

"I'm gonna be a big help. You'll see."

"Mark, I think it's fine if you and Nathan want to work here. Now what was I looking for…?"

Mark's heart lurched. What if she went into a memory lapse that took her to the past? What if she became confused and Nathan went home and told his grandmother? Or more likely, announced it to the whole village? Nathan was a great kid, but he gave the town crier a run for his money. Mark stepped toward his mother hoping to avert disaster.

"Ah, I remember. You like the mug with the bear on it don't you, Nathan?" Minette handed Nathan a cup of milk along with two sugar cookies. Mark sank into the nearest chair, his knees too weak to hold up his overworked brain.

"Whaddya say we go up to Clavier's first, and then we'll circle back to your house for your lesson?" He asked Nathan.

Nathan's mouth was too full of cookie to answer, but he nodded so hard Mark thought his head would snap off.

Ten minutes later, Mark kissed his mom goodbye and left with Nathan beside him. He'd already worked at Clavier's statue twice since finding his father's note. Mark had just assumed maintaining the beacon was his job until his father's return, but he would have liked to have been asked. Was that his father's plan? To leave him with all the responsibilities so he had no choice? Mark's lips tightened with anger.

"When I told Lisa I was helping you, she really wanted to come too," Nathan said. "But I told her she couldn't unless you said so, even though she's my very best friend. Am I your best friend?"

Mark wanted to laugh, but he was careful to only smile. He had to give Nathan credit. He wasn't shy. "I don't think you've ever met my best friend."

"Why not? Does he live somewhere else?"

"Uh, that's a good question, and the answer is yes and no."

"How can it be both?"

"Do you have any friends in your dreams?" Mark asked, actually curious.

"Yeah, of course! But Lisa's still my best, best friend. Does your friend live in your dreams?"

Mark just nodded, not sure how much more he wanted to say.

"What's his name?"

"Shift."

"What's his favorite color?"

"I'll have to ask him. I'm not sure he sees colors the same way we do. He's not human." Nathan was hooked, and Mark was surprised that he was having fun talking about Shift. "In fact he's a different animal every night—or at least part of him is."

Nathan's eyes went wide, and he was lost in silent thought for at least five steps. Mark couldn't remember that ever happening before.

"None of my friends can do that. I can see why he's your best friend," Nathan said, awe in his voice. "If only half of him changes what's the rest of…"

Once they reached the Beacon, Mark went to work. True to his promise, Nathan was a big help: Mark couldn't answer Nathan's constant questions about Shift and think about his father at the same time. And Nathan was also right about something else.

"Shift is the best best friend anyone could have," he announced.

"I couldn't have said it better myself," Mark agreed. *And what am I going to do without him?* He thought. Mark swallowed hard.

He knelt to Nathan's height, and looked him in the eye. "So Shift is our secret, right Nathan? That means you don't talk about him with anyone but me. Cross your heart and promise in front of Clavier."

"I promise," Nathan said, solemn eyes glued to Clavier.

Mark made his own silent promise to Clavier that he'd do his best for his mom and for Shift. "Okay then, let's see how bad your grandmother's cookies really are."

Nick's Nightmare

Nick falls into his familiar nightmare. As always, he floats in black so black he can't see the whiskers on his face. The dark stretches in every direction. He wants to run until he finds the edge of the dark, where he can slip over into the light of day that must be waiting. But there's no ground to push off, and his legs can't propel him forward or back, up or down.

Every hair on his body begins to tingle, and BOOM! Stars break out all around him, turning the black into a spectacular night sky. One star in the distance begins to pulse brighter than the rest. A heartbeat later, like a flame riding the breeze, another light flares to the right of the first, and another…until there are nine pulsing stars strewn out ahead of him.

Nick can feel his lives calling him, and he doesn't know how, but he's moving toward them. He feels like he's swallowed a barrelful of the best-ever catnip. He begins to laugh out loud, because he knows that any wish he can think up will come true when he reaches those stars: Fresh fish, sweet warm cream, a swanky new home and…against all odds, and a lifetime of disappointment, hope kindles inside him.

"Nine brilliant stars are what I see too."

Rose! Nick can't see her, but she's here. That's never happened before. Maybe everything will be different this time. Maybe this time he'll crossover into another life.

A sickening stench hits Nick's nose and leaves his eyes watering. Almost instantly, his stomach rolls over in the hope of retching, but it can't. When his eyes refocus, his nine stars are gone, blotted out by the familiar shape that has swooped into place between he and his lives. Millions of stars have disappeared behind a shadow the size of a mountain range. Nick knows this creature too well: the nauseating lurch, so wrong for waking life, the smoking drool dripping from harpy jaws. Without looking, he knows hundreds of scars mar her hide, where the monstrous creature's skeleton shows through. Her claws are serrated blades, and as she flies, they open and close with a shriek of metal on metal.

She swings around to face them.

Nick hears Rose's strangled mew. He wants to comfort her and tell her that eventually they'll wake up and it will all be over. But his heart is pounding and his voice is broken. And that's the least of his worries, because he can't move, and they have nowhere to hide.

The creature's malicious eyes bore into Nick's. Despite his terror, Nick has the giddy thought of making introductions: "Rose, meet my nightmare. Nightmare, leave Rose alone."

Then the creature turns to Nick's stars.

With a slow and deliberate shove, she stabs a steel claw into the first of Nick's nine stars. Nick feels a searing pain in his chest as the glow flickers, and then dies. He feels the star crumble and fall from the sky.

Nick has learned to close his eyes. It's the one thing he can do. But he still feels the monster destroy the next star, and the next, until he can feel the moment when the last star dies—and his hope with it.

"Rose, we're going to wake up now, it's over," he whispers, sagging with relief.

"I don't think so," Rose says.

Nick opens his eyes. He's still suspended in space. But now he can see Rose facing him across a gap of darkness as wide as Adele's backyard. Nick follows her gaze down. The harpy is grinning up at him as she begins to spin faster and faster beneath Nick and Rose. She opens her rotting jaws, revealing a whirlpool of reeking, tumbling shapes. Instantly, Nick can feel the pull of an undertow, a terrifying new twist on his nightmare.

"Nick, you can fight it." But Rose's voice is filled with terror.

Nick can't respond, mesmerized by the dark shapes of captive beasts swirling beneath them. The whirlpool pulls them closer.

"You don't have to give up and die now," Rose urges.

The nightmare creature tilts her head to one side. Her gaping jaw widens at Rose's thoughts, as if she knows Nick better than anyone else—knows he can't escape her. Oily tendrils appear at the mouth of the whirlpool. One lashes up at Nick, smacking his right rear paw. The paw goes numb. He and Rose fall another few feet, narrowing their distance from the whirlpool to two yards.

Rose falters between words. "Losing…my…grip."

Nick drags his head up to look at her. This is his nightmare, his damaged life, not hers. She's only here because of him. Nick locks his blue eyes to Rose's green, and joins her will to move them up and away from the yawning mouth. Together they begin to rise until they are out of the reach of the tentacles.

"We have to break free, Nick."

Nick nods and calls for all the remaining energy in his body and mind. But three days of cold and lack of food are too many. His energy falters.

As if sensing its moment, the harpy whirlpool surges toward them with a pull so strong that Nick and Rose are stopped, unable to do anything more than hold their place.

"Rose, leave!" Nick grunts.

Rose's eyes tell him she won't.

The undertow drags them down, inch-by-inch. Nick knows Rose's only chance is for him to choose the whirlpool. If he gives the monster what she wants, maybe Rose can escape.

"When…I…say…'go'—"

"Do…you…feel…that?" Rose's teeth are gritted.

And Nick can feel a tiny flame of new energy in his body. He and Rose know who has given them a final chance. They begin to claw at the black sky, climbing, fighting the pull of the hungry jaws.

Out of the Night

Smoke kept watch in the snow beside Nick and Rose. He leapt to his feet when the two unconscious cats whined in fear, their whiskers shuddering. Nick's right back leg twitched once and went limp.

"Come back, Rose! Come back now," Smoke begged. He saw no sign that she heard him. He lay down beside her, giving all he had left, his love, and the fading warmth of his body.

Rose and Nick awoke minutes before full dark. Smoke purred in relief while he confirmed they were uninjured, and then led them into a rocky hollow space nearby. There was no food to share, and fear had sapped their energy. Nick and Smoke curled up on each side of Rose. Smoke was asleep in seconds.

Nick looked at Rose. "I'm sorry. For everything—"

Rose interrupted him. "I don't know if I could live, with that horror waiting for me each time I closed my eyes. Just rest now if you can."

Nick shuddered once, and then fell asleep without any sign of distress.

Rose felt hollow with exhaustion, but she couldn't sleep. Her stomach throbbed with hunger, her muscles were clenched with the effort to keep warm, and her paws were raw from days of walking in snow. She hadn't been able to dreamdance normally since the first terror of being grabbed from behind and tossed into Bart's filthy sack.

Minutes stretched into an hour, then two, and Rose's thoughts were the darkest she could ever remember. Nick's dream had convinced her that she knew far too little about life and dream and her "gift." The nine beckoning stars in Nick's dream were familiar to her from traveling to other cats' lives, yet she didn't seem to have nine specific lives that belonged to her. She didn't know what happened when a dreamdancer died, but she did know that Smoke and Nick were running out of time in their last lives.

What if she had the power to save them, and she just didn't know it?

Smoke awoke beside her, and stretched out a paw. She knew his thoughts mirrored her own. "No sight or scent of a town," she whispered. "We can't last much longer."

"Dying isn't so bad, Rose." Smoke turned his gaze toward the opening, so close, yet almost invisible in the dark. "And each life leaves behind a magical place inside us that is both thrilling and sad at the same time." He turned back to her. "But I hope you won't discover I'm right for many years."

Rose leaned over and licked Smoke's furry face. He smiled sadly, but he drifted back into sleep beneath her strokes. She looked toward the entry hole, noticing the eerie silence.

The wind had been howling a minute ago, but now there was none. The green-eyed cat tilted her head and perked her ears. She heard sleepy breathing, and…singing. Outside, a male voice crooned an ancient melody. Rose leaned toward the voice. Disentangling herself from Smoke and Nick, she stepped from their rocky refuge into the night.

The storm still raged all around her—except in the space between Rose and the bearded singer. He stood three feet in front of Rose, his kind green eyes looking into hers as he sang. He stood, tall and thin in a red cloak, with a coarse green sack slung over one shoulder. Rose felt her heart unknot, and then his song came to an end.

"Father Christmas…" Rose whispered, and then she faltered. She wanted to tell him everything: Adele leaving, Bart's betrayal; how sad she felt for Smoke and Nick; and that she was afraid to die.

Father Christmas smiled down at Rose, nodding silently as if he knew every thought, every feeling. He beckoned Rose closer, dropped his sack to the snow and knelt down beside her to rummage through it. A broad smile lit his bearded face as he pulled his arm from the sack and opened his weathered hand.

A sparkling star hovered above Father Christmas's palm. The dancing fire within the star lit Rose's face with warm light. She purred, looking from the gleaming treasure to Father Christmas's gentle eyes, and back. The star pulsed brighter. Starlight flowed over Rose, carrying her up and up into the night sky.

Rose floated above a candlelit mountain village. A ruby-red beacon shone high on a hilltop above the scene, and she saw tendrils of smoke rising from chimneys, but no people. This was the haven she and Nick and Smoke had been searching for since they'd been abandoned. The quiet scene seemed too perfect to live anywhere outside a dream. But Rose knew the village was real. She heard a female voice, as if the woman floated beside her.

"Just a little further, Rose. You must wake the others and continue. Now."

The next instant, Rose was back in the snow, looking up into the smiling face of Father Christmas. He winked and placed the star in the snow at Rose's paws. Reaching out, he placed three gentle fingers to the white fur over Rose's heart. Warmth and comfort spread through her from his touch to the tip of her grey tail, reclaiming her from the killing cold.

Father Christmas stroked her once in farewell. He stood, took up his sack and began to shimmer and fade. Within moments, Rose could see through his red cloak. Then he was gone.

"Just a little further," came the woman's whisper.

For several moments, Rose could not pull her gaze from the spot where Father Christmas had disappeared. When she finally looked down at the star, she saw that the snow beneath it had melted. She smelled something rich and promising.

Rose awoke back among the damp rocks of their meager shelter, Smoke and Nick curled against her. "Oh," she whispered as she looked around. "Oh," she repeated, her voice heavy with disappointment. "Such a wonderful dream…I still feel warm."

She closed her eyes to hold on to the memory of Father Christmas's caress. She took a deep breath and opened her eyes.

Echoing her dream, Rose moved to the opening. At least the storm really had stopped. She stepped out into a star-studded night, looking up at the sky with new longing. Then she moved to the spot in the snow where Father Christmas had knelt beside her. A golden beehive, dripping with honey gleamed in the snow. One taste told Rose, this was no ordinary gift.

"G'way, Rose, need sleep." Nick burrowed deeper into Smoke's grey fur.

"Too dark, to…" Smoke had already fallen back asleep.

"Smoke, Nick. Believe me, you don't want to miss this." Rose nudged the groggy males up and outside. All three cats fell on the food and ate until they were revived and giddy with happiness. Nick and Smoke had questions.

"How did you find the hive?" Smoke asked.

Rose paced, eager to move on. She could feel the shining beacon pulling her forward.

"Now that we're up, where are we going?" added Nick.

"Just a little further," she said, as she turned to lead the way.

An hour later, Rose crested a steep hill in the road. "Smoke, Nick! Look!" Shoulder to shoulder, Smoke and Nick came up beside her.

In the valley below, moonlight glittered on the frozen river, a shining ribbon weaving among candlelit cabins. Their voices were tight with cold and exhaustion, but all three cats broke into ragged purrs of happiness.

"We made it," said Smoke.

"I don't know how you did it, Rose, but…" Nick's voice trailed off, his eyes locked on the village. The mouth-watering aroma of roasting meat and Christmas spices was undeniable.

"And from the smell of it, you may even get your wish to sit beside a warm fire on Christmas day."

Rose grinned. She recognized the village and the ruby-red beacon on the opposite hilltop. A wave of gratitude rolled through her for Father Christmas and the mysterious woman who'd guided them here.

"Just a little further," she said for the last time.

The exhausted trio stumbled down the hill and into the snow-hushed streets of Dreamhaven.

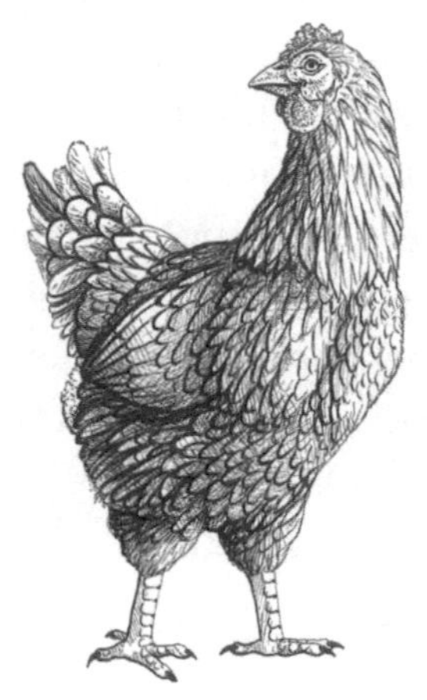

CHAPTER TWENTY-EIGHT

Malicious Marauders

Other unexpected visitors had reached Dreamhaven a few days before the cats, and they'd taken up residence in the home of Eva, the village's industrious laundress. She was a cheerful woman, with hands and feet a bit oversized for her height. But Eva's sturdy body served her well, whether in her hard work each day or out on the dance floor. She often hummed a lively melody as she washed, dried and folded all the laundry villagers and visitors brought to her door. And she always greeted customers with a lively, "Come in, come in. What have you brought me today?" Often friends stayed to chat as the laundress ironed every wrinkle from their shirts and spotless hankies.

But tonight Eva was definitely not cheerful. Though it was after midnight, she sat wide-awake and miserable in her disheveled bed. For the third night in a row, she could not sleep. And in Dreamhaven sleeplessness was unknown. In fact, the village was famous for three things: deep sleep, remarkable dreams and the Fabulous Frozen Fantasma.

Yet Eva sat in her crumpled bed, bleary-eyed, exhausted and too tired to wash, sort or fold. Even the thought of her heavy iron left her limp.

Overwhelmed by growing piles of dirty laundry, Eva had hidden them throughout her house, as far away as possible from the eyes—and noses—of her customers. The fastidious laundress was horrified at the odor spreading through her house. Now she sat wide-awake, her last clean hankie pressed to her besieged nose.

She confessed aloud to no one, "Closing up an hour early today may delay the inevitable, but soon every nose in the village will know: I've got dirty blouses and cuffs in the bathtub, a soaring stack of shirts in the pantry, and a pile of stinky socks beneath the Christmas tree. If I can't get some rest, and do my work, Father Christmas will never set foot in this house." The poor woman began to cry in weary frustration.

But there were twenty-five very good reasons why Eva was sleepless.

"Give me that!" screamed Medusa, snatching a Christmas cookie from an overturned tin in Eva's pantry.

"No. It's mine," snarled a white-freckled male weasel.

"And now it's MINE," chuckled Rogo as he stole the cookie

from Medusa.

Exactly three nights before, Eva had stepped out of her cottage with a washtub, leaving the door ajar behind her. She was outside only long enough to scour the tub with snow, and to notice the gathering clouds of another storm.

But she did not notice twenty-five pairs of ravenous weasel eyes watching her from the trees.

"Splooooosh" As snow poured from Eva's metal washtub, Rogo gave the signal. The boogle raced toward the laundress' candlelit house.

Eva returned inside and closed the door, unaware of her uninvited guests. She blew out the candles and went to bed. And that night, for the first time in her life, Eva did not fall asleep the moment her brown curls touched her delicious goose-down pillow. Each time she'd drift off to sleep, she'd start awake, hearing unusual sounds in the cottage. But each time she sat up and lit the candlestick beside her bed, the noises stopped. Over and over that night, the little woman pushed back her covers, stepped into her wool slippers and trudged through the house, candle held high. And each time, all twenty-five weasels melted into the shadows, exchanging silent sneers at the woman's distress. Finally, Eva gave up and pulled her thick blankets over her head.

The first night the weasels ran from room to room, squabbling over the food stored in Eva's pantry, and the popcorn garlands strung around her Christmas tree. The next night, emboldened by their easy success, the boogle gnawed at a corner of Eva's wooden porch door until they could slip in and out. The third night they fanned out through the village to other homes and shops.

"…and make sure you bring the best loot back here to Headquarters," Rogo demanded. "Let's see what the Dreamhaveners have made us for Christmas."

By day, the weasels hid at the laundress' house, sleeping off their stolen meals behind bookshelves, beneath laundry baskets and inside the boot cupboard. And each night they awoke to overrun the village.

To their delight, the woman had lost her appetite, and was so tired and distracted that she never stepped into her pantry to discover the oatmeal spilled across the wooden floor, the cookie crumbs stuffed beneath the broom, or the cunning holes gnawed into the back of the maple sugar sack.

Each night, the rapacious weasels reveled in their attack on Dreamhaven.

"Ohhhh, aren't we clumsy," they sniggered as they played tag among a villager's fine china teacups, until the sugar bowl toppled and cracked. The wily weasels swished their tails from side to side, spreading the sugar to cover their tracks.

"Hah-hah," they sneered in another cottage, ripping pages from baby books and stealing cheese from the larder. Two of them had returned with a shiny watch on a chain.

"And don't forget those pretty packages," snarled Rogo. He whipped the boogle into a frenzy, insisting they chew through the paper and ribbons on the Christmas gifts tucked beneath the villagers' modest trees.

As the third night wore on, the boogle reassembled at Eva's, passing the time by reducing her lovingly wrapped presents to tattered bows and shredded paper.

While the laundress tossed and turned upstairs in her bedroom, the weasels grew bored. Looking for new diversions, they shoved the thinnest weasel through the gap beneath the door to the basement.

"I can see a long table and...piles of clean stuff," he reported back from the top of the basement steps.

"They won't be clean for long," sneered Rogo. He leapt up and hooked his front paws over the basement door handle. With his weight, the door unlatched and swung open. "Follow me," Rogo barked as he led the pack down the stairs.

CHAPTER TWENTY-NINE

First Encounter

The cats reached the trees beside the nearest cottage, and sat in the shadows to study the building and get a sense of the village. After several minutes, Smoke rose and padded around the far corner to see what was nearby. "Rose, Nick, over here!" He called.

The excitement in Smoke's voice was irresistible, and as they turned the corner, they found him standing beside a wide wooden door. "Look! This door is open a crack, and I can see firelight through that window. Let's see what's in there. Maybe we can get out of the cold."

The three friends stepped up to the door, taking turns to

peek around the edge. The firelight came from a furnace. Only a few feet away, four wicker baskets overflowed with clean, white sheets atop a long worktable.

"I could sure use a few hours of warm napping," said Nick.

"Let's go in," Rose agreed.

All three cats leaned their weight against the door and pushed into the gap repeatedly. The crack inched open until it gaped wide enough for them to enter. Nick shoved past to be first into the cozy basement.

He looked up to see a stream of weasels cascading down the steps. The weasels froze at the sight of him, but their leader recovered first.

"No stinking cat is going to poach in our territory," he snarled in a low voice to the surrounding pack. He looked directly into Nick's eyes "Thanks for delivering fresh meat to Headquarters," he taunted the startled cat. "Come on, let's get him."

Nick knew from experience, that despite their small size, weasels were fierce and deadly fighters. They swarmed toward him. Nick felt Rose enter the basement with Smoke on her heels. They aligned beside him to meet the first wave of attack.

With the sudden appearance of two additional fighters, the leader and his top four lieutenants surged forward, but the rest of the boogle had a change of heart. They scrambled, reversing their path to race back up the steps. They fled the laundress' house at top speed, scattering in every direction. Sensing disarray behind him, the lead weasel veered right, leaping from floor to tabletop, his army evaporating around him. "Retreat! Retreat!" he screamed to the remaining weasels, but Nick had made short work of two of them and was already mid-leap for the worktable. The scarred weasel ran for his life. He fled up the basement steps, Nick gaining ground behind him.

"Rowwwll!" At the sound of a cat in pain, Nick broke off the chase, spun on his rear legs and sped back to the fight in the basement. He didn't wait to watch the lead weasel scramble out the nearest exit.

By the time Nick reached the bottom step, the battle was over. Four weasels lay dead, including the two Nick had killed. Rose was licking a bite on Smoke's tail clean.

"Some welcoming party!" Smoke said, as Nick walked over to examine the wound. "But we won." Smoke said, proud of fighting off their attackers.

"At least for tonight," agreed Nick. He'd seen the cold cruelty in the ugly weasel's eyes, and he felt certain the boogle leader would be back for revenge. "I think that bite will heal fine," he finished.

"What if these are the humans' pets?" asked Rose, looking at the weasel bodies. "If they are, we won't be welcome here."

"We don't know they belong to the humans," said Smoke.

Nick snorted. "Well, there were a heck of a lot of them dancin' down the stairs to go unnoticed by the owner," he said, washing blood from his left forepaw.

"But isn't that far too many anything to keep as pets?" asked Smoke.

"Just in case, I think we'd better hide the evidence," Rose said. "And I don't want to sleep in this mess anyway."

Nick and Smoke nodded silent agreement. By the time the cats had satisfied their hunger, their adrenaline had worn off. Despite numbing fatigue, they dragged the remains outside and hid them in the woods. Nick yawned as they re-entered the basement.

"Right now, I don't care about weasels or humans. I'm going to bed down in those sheets," he said.

Smoke and Rose joined him as he jumped up onto the work-table. Fifteen minutes later, the cats had licked away most of their travel and battle stains. Together they stepped into a basket, curled up and settled in for a well-earned rest. Each had painful reminders of the journey: exhaustion, raw paws, Smoke's bite and multiple bits of missing fur. But for now, the three friends were safe. Tucked in among the folds of soft sheets, Rose and Smoke fell into deep sleep.

And so did Nick.

CHAPTER THIRTY

Eva's Dream

Upstairs, Eva also finally fell asleep and into a vivid dream: It was night and Christmas Eve. The laundress left her bedroom to go downstairs. Her Christmas tree stood in its usual place beside the window, but the dirty socks piled beneath the tree were gone. In fact, in her dream, she knew that the dirty laundry throughout the house had disappeared.

"Gone, it's all gone!" laughed Eva with relief and delight.

Just then, three dream cats stepped out from behind the Christmas tree. Each cat stood upright on rear paws, wearing a jewel colored jacket with brass cat eye buttons. Eva could hear the cats purring as they lined up before her, paws extended. The smiling female cat had green eyes to match her jade green jacket, and held out a lace pillow.

"For me?" Eva asked with shy surprise, hugging the pillow to her heart.

The gray cat was very handsome in his red jacket as he placed a sky-blue blanket around Eva's shoulders with gentle care.

"Why, it's soft as a kitten," sighed Eva.

The blue-furred cat looked remarkable in his purple jacket. He offered Eva a steaming cup of her favorite tea, and then slipped a pair of tasseled slippers onto her feet.

"Oh my," the little laundress said.

Then all three felines were holding a white cloud stretched between them. Accepting their smiling invitation, Eva curled up on the exotic mattress, and let the cats float her up the stairs and right to her bed.

The next morning, Eva awoke rejuvenated and energetic. "What a fabulous dream! I feel wonderful. I must get right to work."

And she did. Eva knew, that thanks to her dreamy feline friends, she would have her house ready in time to welcome Father Christmas. She remained busy all day upstairs, with no thought to spare for the sheets in the basement. Eva never knew that her dream cats were asleep right beneath her feet.

Explorers

Outside, the waxing December moon had not yet risen, and the village streets were dark and quiet. Inside the cabins and cottages of Dreamhaven, adults throughout the village were busy with bedtime chores.

Nathan's grandmother answered yet another of his questions. "Don't worry, Nathan. Even if we haven't caught the thieves and hooligans by then, on Christmas Eve, Father Christmas will come right into the village, and…"

"…and then he'll visit our house," Joycelyn promised her drooling baby, Stephan, in a cottage on the east edge of the village.

"…but only if no more of our china teacups turn up broken," Angela Del'arte teased her husband, Robert. He was adding the finishing touches to his latest automaton, a seal riding a bicycle.

"That wasn't me, Angela. Honest," Robert protested.

"Please bring my father home for my mother's sake, Father Christmas," Mark whispered at his loft window.

At last, straggling arms and legs were tucked beneath downy quilts, a great many goodnight kisses were exchanged and bedroom candles were blown out. As the children drifted off to sleep, the grownups returned to the fireside to put final touches to presents that would soon lie beneath the Christmas tree. The quiet grew deep as the hours passed, until even the adults could no longer stifle their yawns. Banking the fires, they made their way to bed.

Nick, Rose and Smoke awoke in the laundress' basement. They'd slept through the entire day, and they enjoyed the luxury of warmth and slow grooming. The unexpected weasel meat had replenished their strength, and the night's solid rest had begun to heal their wounds.

"Wow, that was some nap," said Nick, licking the fur at the tip of his tail.

"Mmmmm," agreed Smoke mid-stretch, "I'll take soft sheets over rocks and pinecones any day. How about you, Rose?"

"It was delicious. I feel much better," she answered. "But I bet someone comes for these cozy sheets tomorrow."

"So tonight's our chance to explore the village and find a new—" Smoke broke off, thinking about Adele. He looked at Rose with silent chagrin.

But before she could respond, Nick spoke between licks of his outstretched right rear paw. "I'm not so sure I'd want to settle here long term," he said.

Smoke and Rose stopped grooming to look at Nick.

His paw still suspended in mid-air, he looked up to find their eyes on him. He dropped his paw and sat up to face his friends. "Maybe those weasels are the human's pets. Or maybe they've just arrived in the village. Either way, they're a problem. We were lucky last night, but we can't keep fighting them, without …consequences."

"You mean casualties," said Rose.

The silence in the basement was loud.

"We need to know more about them," Nick said. "One of the weasels called the leader 'Rogo.' What if you stepped into Rogo's dreams, Rose? Maybe you'd see his plans."

"Rogo seems filled with hate. Even in dream, hate is a powerful emotion, and it can be contagious. I'd rather not dreamdance him, unless there's absolutely no other way."

"We have to find food, and we need to know more about the village," said Smoke.

Nick nodded. "Together we're safer, but we can't cover as much ground. And we're also more likely to be seen."

"Let's split up tonight to learn everything we can about the village," said Rose. "Then we make our next decisions—whether we stay, or how and when we're going to leave."

"Like I said before, we don't know the weasels are welcome here either," said Smoke.

"Well if they aren't, this town could sure use some good cats," laughed Nick. In the face of his friends' enthusiasm, he silenced his misgivings. "Okay, if we reach the center of the village without a weasel fight, we split up."

Rose and Smoke nodded. Nick jumped down from the table, and led them from the comfort of the warm basement into the streets of Dreamhaven.

Even with the benefit of a fine coat of cat fur, the night felt quite chilly. The friends stepped from shadow to shadow moving toward the middle of the village. Ten minutes later, they hadn't met a single soul, human or weasel. They stopped in front of a candlelit shop. An impressive sign in red and gold lettering hung above the brass-handled door:

Robert Del'arte – A Magician's Best Friend
Inventor of
Illusions, Vanishings, Magical Mechanicals & Automatons

Two large windows flanked the front door. The cats could see that the living spaces were on the upper floor, while the entire bottom floor was devoted to the shop. In the nearest window, a golden birdcage held a mechanical peacock that dangled a brilliant tail of iridescent blues and greens.

"I know he's not real, but he is impressive," said Rose.

"Come look at this window," Nick called.

In the second window, Robert Del'arte was tracing Father Christmas's journey to Dreamhaven. Thirty-one oil lights, each shining through a crystal star, were strung across the window at different heights. The tiny lights sent a soft glow over the winter scene.

"It looks like stars are shining inside the shop," purred Rose.

Hand-painted mountains surrounded a small, perfect model of Dreamhaven. The doors of each miniature building opened on brass hinges, and, very like the real village, the windows of the little homes revealed tiny Christmas trees.

"Look, there's the beacon, and there's the inn, and wow, the mill wheel really turns," laughed Smoke.

The small streets were filled with snow made of white cotton streaked with silver threads that glistened in the starlight.

"I don't see Father Christmas," said Nick. "Where is he?"

"I've seen something like this in Adele's dreams. Father Christmas can't appear in the scene until Christmas morning," answered Rose. "But see his footprints—there, and over there? I bet you that on the first of December, that tiny pair of green boot prints appeared in the distant mountains. And then every few days, new prints have appeared, always larger and closer to the village. Christmas is only three days away, and over there, in the paper forest beside the village, there are two bigger footprints."

Nick and Smoke followed her gaze and nodded their understanding, enjoying the details of the miniature scene.

"Look! All along his way here, Father Christmas has been giving gifts," said Smoke.

In the mountains, a yawning bear peeked from the depths of his den. The bear, just two inches tall, was so well carved and painted that he looked ready to talk to the cats. A pile of bright berries and a sprig of holly lay at his feet.

"He's great," said Nick.

"But I'm glad we didn't meet the real thing on our way here," said Smoke.

At the river, Father Christmas had placed a crunchy red cinnamon stick atop the beaver family's lodge. Further down the mountain, a raccoon and three kits gobbled corn kernels scattered in the snow, while on a branch overhead, a handsome black squirrel clutched an acorn tied with a green satin bow. Rabbits sat in the cotton snow feasting on fresh carrots with green leafy tops, beside a red fox licking at a glazed ham.

"Good thing for the rabbits Father Christmas remembered to feed the fox too," said Rose.

Closest to the village, a family of deer peeked from behind paper trees, as they munched sheaves of fresh, succulent grass and fresh roses.

"Look, Father Christmas is coming the same way we did," said Nick. "How come we didn't meet up with him? How come he didn't find us?"

"We did meet Father Christmas on our journey," Rose said quietly, her eyes still on the window.

"What? When?" said Nick and Smoke at the same time.

"How come I didn't see him?" asked Nick. "Did you see him, Smoke?"

"No, I didn't. But I secretly hoped he'd find us."

"I promise to tell you all about it—tomorrow," laughed Rose seeing their expressions. "Because tonight we explore. Right?"

Nick felt torn between hearing about Father Christmas, and using every minute to investigate the village. "Right," he finally conceded. "And tomorrow, we hide during the day—"

"And then we meet back here, same time tomorrow night," put in Smoke.

"Okay," said Rose, taking a deep breath.

Their plan was complete, but no one moved. When falling snow from a nearby tree branch broke the silence, Nick rose to his feet.

"I'll meet you here tomorrow night," he promised. Then he trotted off toward the nearest lane, his rear paws propelling him into the black beyond the post office, leaving small v's in the snow.

Smoke brushed lovingly against Rose, and she sensed that he was mostly excited, with a dash of fear—for her.

"If we stay together, we can keep each other company," Smoke said.

Rose looked across the short gap between them, never allowing her green eyes to waver from Smoke's worried ones. "If we're going to find out as much as possible, we've got to split up."

For a moment, Smoke looked up at the inventor's window. When he looked back, he'd reached his decision. "Then I guess that's my cue." He stepped close to his sister, gave her nose a gentle bump and cocked his head. "Promise me you'll be careful."

"I will if you will." Rose nodded once, and Smoke moved off in fluid grace, a grey memory against the white snow.

Five long minutes passed. Rose looked to the left of the illusionist's shop, directly at Smoke's hiding place beneath the tall fir tree.

"I'll miss you, Smoke," she called. "And I'll see you tomorrow." She smiled at Smoke's disgruntled snort. Then she turned her paws toward the heart of Dreamhaven.

Clavier's Beacon

Rose moved with cautious haste, sticking to the shadows, but always climbing up and eastward. Twenty minutes after leaving Smoke in front of the illusionist's shop, she sat in the snow beneath the ruby-red beacon. The domed oil light lay cradled in the bronze palm of a bigger than life-size statue. A smiling woman in a long traveling cloak stood proud and welcoming atop a stone pedestal carved with a single name: CLAVIER.

Rose saw Clavier's open arms and the fresh crown of green and red holly atop her flowing bronze hair. Though Clavier was a statue, Rose knew that somehow she had guided Rose through the dark to Dreamhaven.

"Thank you for helping us, Clavier," Rose whispered, looking up into the bronze face.

Clavier's metallic skin softened and melted away. In moments, a human woman with smiling green eyes, and a thick gray braid stood smiling down at Rose.

"You're most welcome, Rose," Clavier answered in her resonant voice. "Shall we get better acquainted?"

"I'd like that," Rose nodded.

Still holding the beacon high, Clavier extended her free hand to Rose. The dreamdancer jumped into Clavier's palm, and climbed to the woman's shoulder to settle in among the soft folds of her hood. For over an hour, they talked, learning about each other's lives. Then Clavier shared a secret.

"There's an enchantment on the village?" Rose repeated.

"Yes. The village has been enchanted and under my protection for several centuries," said Clavier. "Would you like to know more about Dreamhaven?" She nodded toward the red beacon in her palm.

Rose, felt willing to linger in Clavier's tender warmth forever. "Yes, please."

"So be it." Clavier whispered, looking into the ruby light in her palm.

As the green-eyed cat leaned forward to watch, the red light crackled and shone even brighter. The village below glowed and the whole valley wavered.

Rose came to her feet on Clavier's shoulder. "What about Smoke and Nick?" she asked.

"No one in the village will be harmed by the time shift. I promise they won't even notice."

In an instant, the transformation was complete: The valley

below them now held no more than a dozen rough cottages on one side of the river. There were more trees, but no bridge, inn or shops. Storm winds pounded down the valley, lashing the trees from side to side, hurling snow at the handful of homes.

"Dreamhaven," Rose whispered.

"Aaah, but the village wasn't called 'Dreamhaven' then. We've moved back in time over three hundred years, a time when a kind of madness gripped much of the world. Some leaders believed that evil lived inside anyone creative or different. They were wrong, but they had an excuse for cruelty and war. No one felt safe. Fear became the norm. Too many innocent people, and some of the world's most beautiful dreams were shattered and broken." Clavier took a deep breath before continuing.

"In those dark times, I was asked to find a place where dreams would be safe. If we could not save people, we would seek a place of kindness where their dreams of truth and beauty would have a chance to grow strong, and wait for the world to change. We hoped that one day beautiful dreams would again be free to find the beings they were born to inspire, so that dreams and dreamers could once more fulfill their entwined destinies."

"And you accepted the job," said Rose.

"You're right, I did. And I asked the two people I loved most to join me. We searched for more than two years through remote, uncharted lands. It was November, and we still had not found the right place. And then, on a lovely winter day, we were caught in an avalanche. My companions were killed."

Clavier's voice broke. Rose turned from watching the village to see tears sliding down the woman's wrinkled cheek. She leaned against Clavier's neck in silent comfort. Clavier stroked Rose in gratitude.

"I was injured, utterly lost and very near the end of my

strength…"

A cloaked figure appeared in the ancient village.

Staggering against the force of the wind-whipped snow, a woman emerges from the trees. She falls to the ground. On hands and knees she crawls to the door of the nearest cottage.

"Help! Please help!" Her weak words are barely audible, torn away by the howling wind. The door opens a crack. Then a white-haired couple rush to draw the prostrate woman into their home.

The seasons change. Winter white melts to reveal forests of new green and mountain meadows covered in yellow, pink and purple wild-flowers. The sun is brilliant in the sky, and the river shines and gurgles against its banks. Clavier, her health restored, carries a walking stick in one hand, and a small sack of provisions on her back. She turns to the villagers, touching each one with a loving green-eyed gaze. She speaks to them in a clear voice.

"I arrived here helpless and alone with no way to repay you. Yet you shared your precious food, your firesides, and your time with me. In exchange for your kindness and generosity, I now offer something in return: If you wish, tonight and ever after, everyone who sleeps in your village can enjoy deep sleep and magical dreams."

Silence.

Then the children realize what she has said. "Did she say 'magical dreams'?"

But the adults exchange worried glances, and Clavier knows exactly what they are thinking: "It's wonderful that Clavier wants to repay us, but how can anyone fulfill what she's promised?"

But she stands before them, her thick, gray braid entwined with a ribbon of forest green. She smiles and continues. "The dreams come with only one request: that from this day forward, you continue to be kind, working together to solve problems in peaceful ways, and to fulfill each other's finest dreams. I promise that if you do, your dreams will always be beautiful—and inspiring. Do you wish to accept the dreams under these terms?"

The children's votes are loud and unanimous. "Yeaaaahh! Yeaaaahh!"

The adults put their heads together to talk in low voices. Minutes later, they turn to Clavier and answer as one. "We accept."

Clavier, green eyes filled with love and gratitude, bends low to gather all the children to her in one great embrace. "Farewell, and enjoy your sweet dreams," she says, kissing each upturned face. The task she set out to accomplish years before fulfilled, she places her walking stick firmly on the road to begin her journey out of the comfortable village and its quiet valley. The villagers watch her shrink smaller with the growing distance between them. She turns to wave once more, and then Clavier disappears from sight.

"Did they do what you asked? Is this where the beautiful dreams came to live?" Rose whispers into Clavier's ear.

"Would you like to find out?" asked Clavier.

"I would," answered Rose, smiling back.

They returned to watching the red globe.

By nightfall, many adults had already forgotten Clavier's promise and her final words. But the children had not.

"Oh, no, Daddy, no more pudding. I have to go to bed. Right now." Four-year old Regina gives her father a sticky goodnight kiss, climbs off his lap, and trots toward her bedroom.

"I think I'll go to bed early tonight," Danny tells his Grandmother.

"Now Danny, we'll have no tantrums. You've got to go to bed at a reasonable hour tonight—what did you say, child?"

"I said, 'goodnight,' Grandma."

She kisses her grandson goodnight, shaking her head in disbelief.

"Goodnight, Mama, Papa, we're very tired." Nellie and Tye hug their stunned parents goodnight.

In every cottage, surprised parents watch their children climb into bed early and unasked. The children do not beg for one more story. Instead, they tuck themselves in to await their enchanted dreams. Some children are so excited that they remain wide-awake for hours. But eventually, sleep claims each and every villager. And the next morning...

"It felt so real. I could feel the wind on my face, every nerve alive. All my life I've dreamed of skiing like that, but I've never believed I could..."

"...and suddenly I understood the formula, and why it was important. I've already filled a notebook. Let me show you..."

"... but this ship was the strangest and most amazing I've ever seen. The sails were different—more this shape. But oh, the way this beauty was balanced. I'm going to build that ship someday."

"The entire story is here in my head. I can't put ink to paper fast enough..."

"...and we don't need to argue over the barn. We can build it to meet all our needs."

Soon the villagers are lending each other tools and encouragement. They're talking over plans for books, for new paintings and enchanting melodies. The village crackles with energy. A full week passes before people return to their regular routines, and several more before they believe their amazing dreams will continue. And, though no one speaks of it, a handful of folks take to napping during the day—just in case.

Over the years, the villagers continue to discover ways to solve their grievances peacefully, and to help each other's dreams come true. Each night, their beautiful dreams return. In honor of Clavier, they erect a statue holding a gleaming red beacon to guide travelers to shelter."

"And so it has been for three centuries," said Clavier. "Until now."

Before Rose could ask what she meant, Clavier continued. "Let's get you back to Smoke and Nick, shall we?" The ancient woman with the ageless smile again concentrated on the ruby beacon, and below them the village wavered and shimmered until the current Dreamhaven was restored.

"So that's how the village earned its name," Clavier said.

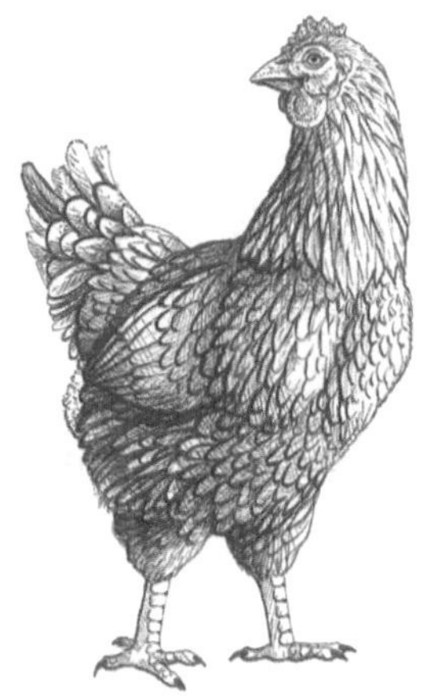

CHAPTER THIRTY-THREE

Without a Net

$\mathcal{D}$arkness fell early on December twenty-second, but firelight danced among the Christmas ornaments on Mark's tree. He'd put away the remains of their cheese-on-toast dinner, cleaned up the dishes and read his history assignment. Then, to cheer his mother, he told her past adventures with Shift. "…so we jumped overboard and the dolphins were right there to meet us. They led us to the secret cove, and Shift and I stayed there until the coast was clear."

Minette sat in the overstuffed chair, gazing into the fire, content to listen. But Mark had to work hard to hide his misery.

Three nights ago they'd decorated the tree—and he'd made the decision to stop dreaming. He'd never been this long without Shift, and he really missed him. And he felt numb from lack of sleep, because he'd spent those long nights in excruciating contortions that defied sleep, or out walking the deserted streets of Dreamhaven. Even so, he'd fallen asleep some, but mostly he'd awakened before he'd begun to dream. Mark didn't know how much longer he could stick to his plan.

Minette stood up. "I'm off to bed. And you should be too," she said. "You look tired."

"I'll just read a little while longer, Mom."

She kissed his fire-warmed hair and stepped into her bedroom.

A half-hour later, Mark felt certain his mother was asleep. He stoked the fire to a comfortable level, and stepped to the hooks in the entry, pulling on his sheep-lined coat, hat, gloves and boots. He paused once to listen, and heard only his mother's even breathing. His exhaustion made his limbs and head feel like thick logs, but Mark stepped out beneath the cloud-covered sky for another nocturnal ramble. The cold would keep him awake, and more importantly, it would keep him anchored in this world.

As he walked, Mark thought again about his father's note and its most disturbing words—the ones that weren't there: "I'll be back soon," or "I'll miss you."

Those words were the reason Mark walked the streets of Dreamhaven in the middle of the night. If his father did come home, Mark had decided to be different. He'd be firmly planted in reality. His father would see that, and together they could take care of his mother. They would be a family again.

His father's voice drifted back to him. "You're even more of a dreamer than your mother. You'll have to wake up someday soon, son."

Until last spring, his mother had smiled reassurance at Mark and chided his father. "Sean, if your dreams were as wonderful as Mark's, you'd want them night and day too."

Mark shivered at the memory, instead of cold. He felt confused. Shift and his dreams had always been wonderful. But now his imagination might be his worst enemy, and his waking life was the scariest place he'd ever known.

"What if my father's right?" he asked the silence. An owl hooted from a tree, but Mark didn't know if that meant "yes" or "no." Since the day he'd come home to his father's note, it seemed as if all he had were questions: What if his mother's childhood dog, Mira, had never been real? Would the dreams he shared with Shift lead him only to confusion like hers? Was he already ill?

From his spot on the path, Mark could see Clavier's beacon blazing high on the hill across the river. What would Clavier say about that? Had she meant for some dreams to be too magical? Was that even possible?

For a single moment, the ruby light seemed to flash. In the next heartbeat, the glow had subsided to normal. As he turned from the light to walk on, Mark felt ashamed. He was worrying about his own problems, when his mother needed him most. He'd think about something besides missing Shift. He'd think about... loyalty.

Mark walked on, urging his mind to review all he knew about loyalty. No one could have a more loyal friend than Shift. Mark began to relive a dream: He and Shift fought side-by-side against hideous gorgons.

"Now you're ugly, and DEAD!" Mark's fantasy sword arced through the air to deliver a fatal blow. He and Shift were hopping in a wild victory dance when he remembered he wasn't supposed to dream—or even think about Shift. And right then, a new question popped into Mark's head. Had his dreams already driven his father away?

The thought stopped Mark in mid-step. Had his father really left them? Two weeks ago, he would never have believed it. But tonight…that was just one more question he couldn't answer. Mark's chest tightened, and he felt like he'd run a mile.

Okay, fine. Perfect. He wasn't sure how much longer he could go on without Shift—or sleep—but a good run would probably leave him too exhausted to dream. Mark took off down the hillside as if a pride of hungry lions was snapping at his heels.

CHAPTER THIRTY-FOUR

Boys in the Bakery

Smoke loped around a corner, to find Nick investigating a slide that started at street level and disappeared beneath the Dreamhaven bakery.

"Smoke, look. I think we can get inside this way. Since you're here, wanna have a look?"

Smoke was on his way to the bridge across the river, but intrigued, he trotted over to inspect Nick's discovery. "I see the gap between the slide and the building, but there's some screening to keep out rodents," he said.

"Yep, and those rodents have already broken through in the corner. With both our weights we can widen it enough to slip underneath."

"Seems to me you've done this before," grinned Smoke.

"Seems to me you're right," Nick smiled back.

The cats didn't know that the miller and his assistant stacked 50-pound bags of flour onto the slide, and the heavy sacks easily slid right down into the baker's kitchen. What they did know was that a little work on the screen, and they were in.

"Hoo-Hoo," laughed Nick as he slid out of sight. Smoke arrived at the bottom a moment later.

"Let's do it again!" Nick crowed.

"Oh, yeaaaah," agreed Smoke. "How should we get back to the top?"

"Aaah, that's easy. We make a running leap to that sack—"

"I think we should…" Smoke interrupted.

Long overdue for fun, they rejected a dozen plans before they agreed on the most complicated. Nick crouched to leap and grab an overhead shelf.

"Not that one, you'll knock over the sack of flou—" but Smoke's warning came too late.

"Sorry. I have to say, you really do look better in grey fur. White's not your color," Nick said through his laughter.

"Huh-huh-shoooo!" Smoke sneezed before he could growl his response.

"But now you won't have to worry about that tricky first step," Nick added as Smoke took a breath to blame him. "Come on! Let's get the pans on the hooks swinging."

"Yeah, if we get them swinging hard enough and time it just right, we should have an easy jump to the windowsill," Smoke agreed, his enthusiasm returning.

"And then it's all downhill from there." The male cats laughed in unison.

Mark stopped running. He took a deep breath and let it out.

"Avoiding dreams in Dreamhaven is stupid," he said aloud. "But as long as I'm out here awake," Mark mimicked his father's cadence, "I've got both feet on the ground. Stupid idea," he said in his own voice.

Mark had reached the village's modest main streets. This late on a winter night, the shop and house windows were all dark, except for the oil candles in Mr. Del'arte's magic shop window. Mark paused to enjoy the miniature village scene. He had all night, and no one would see him because they were all asleep. And dreaming. This was Dreamhaven after all, the place where fantastic dreams were a nightly experience.

Mark felt both brassy and nervous. He knew that his dreams with Shift had emboldened him enough to walk the real streets of Dreamhaven in the dead of night. But if someone did see him, he'd be in trouble. And trouble was the last thing he needed. Just in case, he'd already practiced his excuse. He'd say he was tracking down the mysterious Christmas culprits, and protecting the village. And he was.

With that thought, Mark turned from the candlelit window and headed toward darker shadows. He'd just turned the corner of the bakery, when he saw something move at the top of the delivery slide. Then that something's head swiveled toward Mark, and stared back at him with two glowing eyes. For an instant, animal and boy were frozen in the spotlights of each other's gaze.

In the moonlight, Mark could make out a cat's head and front paws. The chute hid the rest of the body. The animal's pose looked so mischievous and Shift-like that Mark automatically smiled. The feline's head crooked to one side in interest—just like Shift. Mark's smile froze and then went out.

"What if I'm really home in bed and dreaming again?" he thought. What if I can't tell the difference anymore?" He didn't move a muscle. He couldn't risk scaring the animal, if it was a real animal. He needed to know.

"Shift? Is that you?" Mark whispered, his heart beating fast. The cat leaned towards Mark. "Meooowww?"

"Crack!"

Mark jumped, spinning his head toward the river. He was so tense, that the familiar sound of expanding ice on the river was shocking. When he looked back, the slide was empty. He moved to the ramp to look into the kitchen. The slide was as dark as a well, and just as secretive.

"Shift? Shift are you there?" Mark whispered.

CHAPTER THIRTY-FIVE

Problem Pets

High on the hill, Rose and Clavier were discussing Christmas Eve, now only two days away. "I think you'll really enjoy the Fabulous Frozen Fantasma," said Clavier.

"The…what?" Rose asked.

"I'm sure Smoke and Nick will know all about our favorite dessert," laughed Clavier. "It's the other reason Dreamhaven is famous."

"This village is so much more than it seems," Rose said. "It's really nice that the villagers did what you asked. And I'm glad the dreams have a safe place to live. My brother and I and our friend, Nick, have big dreams too, but—" Rose fell silent.

"What's troubling you?" asked Clavier.

Rose raised her head to answer, but for the first time since they'd met, she wasn't sure she should tell Clavier the full reason for her worries. She looked into the woman's kind eyes and made up her mind.

"What if there's no safe place for us in Dreamhaven?"

With a nod Clavier encouraged Rose to continue.

"We're afraid to let the humans know we're here because we've had some bad experiences. And since we arrived…" Rose took a deep breath, knowing she needed to know the truth, even if the answer dashed her hopes. "You say the villagers are kind and the dreams feel safe here. But if they're such nice people, why do they keep such bloodthirsty pets?"

"Bloodthirsty pets? You think Rogo and his boogle belong to the humans?"

Rose nodded. "'Until we met them, we thought surviving the storm was our biggest problem."

"I assure you, the weasels are not pets—or even welcome guests in Dreamhaven. But you should also know that not all of the weasels are cruel. Many are just trying to survive—like you. Unfortunately, they're following a leader who preys on their fear and stirs them to violence."

Rose looked unconvinced.

"Let me show you some more recent Dreamhaven history."

As time shifted in the ruby beacon, Rose leaned forward and recognized the burly weasel from the battle. But the Rogo she saw in the red globe looked younger and had far fewer scars. It was night, and he stood outside a hen house talking to a second, thinner weasel.

"One each? Are you crazy? C'mon let's grab as many as we can.

We'll eat like kings," Rogo urged.

"You can grab as many as you want, Rogo, I don't care. But I like to slip in nice and fast, get my bird for supper, and get outta here before the farmer hears us."

"What? I don't believe my ears." Rogo was angry. "My big strong brother is afraid of a few dumb egg layers and a slow, stupid Dreamer? You should be glad nobody else from the boogle is hearing this, Monty. You're shaming our whole family."

"I'm done talking. Like I said, do what you want, and I'll meet you back at the den."

"Don't worry, I will," Rogo hissed, turning his back on his older brother. "But don't expect me to keep my mouth shut when Dad brags about his son, Monty, 'the best, smartest hunter in the whole boogle.'"

Rogo raced into the henhouse and let his anger fuel his bite, not caring who heard him. Minutes later he struggled to drag two dead chicks through the bushes.

"Blam!" A gun went off, and buckshot whizzed all around him. Rogo opened his jaws and dropped the birds.

"Run, Rogo, run," called Monty from his left.

"Blam!" The gun went off again.

And Rogo did run. All the way back to the weasel den.

"Where's the nice fresh chicken you were bringing for dinner, Rogo?" His mother asked.

"Where's Monty? I thought he was with you," said his father.

"Leave me alone! Just leave. Me. Alone," Rogo snarled.

His parents and relatives were happy to oblige, as he stood just inside the den entrance, snarling and muttering under his breath, his tail swishing back and forth in anger. "C'mon, Monty, c'mon! Quit messin' around, and get back here… that rotten farmer… those stupid Dreamers and their stinkin' chickens…"

Rogo still stood at the entrance to the den when the sun rose.

The beacon resumed its normal glow, and Clavier turned to Rose.

"Rogo's brother died that night. Losing Monty damaged Rogo. And because he's never admitted his part in Monty's death, he's twisted all that festering anger and guilt into one purpose, revenge on Dreamhaven. He's set the boogle loose on the village, and as you know, he has more than Christmas pie and a few ripped ribbons in mind."

"Now that you cats have arrived," Clavier continued, "Rogo is desperate. And he has the potential to affect everyone, including you, and even the dreams."

"We didn't come here to fight," Rose said.

"I know that," said Clavier, stroking Rose's fur. "I also know its no coincidence that Smoke, Nick and you—a powerful dreamdancer—have arrived here now.

For three centuries, the dreams have moved through the world, quietly finding their dreamers. But now, if the world is ready, they will show themselves again. We have a chance for a new age of peace and hope—if we pass the test. Soon, everyone in Dreamhaven will face deep decisions."

Clavier smiled at Rose, but the dreamdancer sensed the woman's worry.

CHAPTER THIRTY-SIX

Bakery Dustup

Nick was shocked at the longing in the human boy's voice. As he began to haul himself up the slide, closer to the boy, the ice cracked. Nick jumped and lost his grip. He tumbled down the slide to the bakery floor and landed on Smoke in a messy heap.

"Ouch! Your foot's in my ear," Smoke said from beneath Nick.

"Hold on…I've got to…there."

"Why'd you crash into me?"

"Didn't you hear the ice shift? That human saw us—"

"Creaaaaaak." The cats froze, eyes moving to the slide. But nothing more happened. They'd just begun to relax, when both cats sniffed the air, and scrambled to fighting stances.

Three weasels, two adults and a young female, appeared from another room of the bakery. But to the cats' surprise, the weasels ignored them. Instead, the three moved to the deep bins of walnuts and pine nuts. They dug in and were soon crunching full mouthfuls. The cats were stunned. They didn't know that the weasels had spent the day listening to Rogo's version of the Battle of the Blue Beast, until they were convinced that the cats' victory had just been dumb luck, and that every member of the boogle was a hero.

"They took us by surprise."

"Next time we'll be ready for 'em."

"You don't need luck when you're really tough," they boasted to each other.

So, instead of attacking Nick and Smoke, the weasels stuffed themselves with nutty treats. There'd be plenty of time to deal with the harmless cats after dinner.

Nick and Smoke stared at the weasels for two heartbeats. Then they signaled each other with a twitch of whiskers. The cats pretended to groom. In truth, they were watching the weasels in stolen glimpses, measuring distances and noting all the exits from the bakery. Each time Nick rolled to reach a new section of fur, he moved a tiny bit closer to the weasel on his left.

Smoke discovered a cat's-eye marble behind an oven paddle.

"Wanna play?" he winked at Nick.

"Ohhhhh. Yeah, sure—if you really want to, but I don't want to work too hard, so keep it nice and eeeeasy," Nick replied.

Pretending boredom, Smoke passed the marble to Nick in a slow, lazy roll. The cats pawed the pretty plaything back and forth, adjusting their positions to catch the marble, the gap between them widening with each pass. The weasels chomped away, their eyes glued to the ball, and their senses dulled by full stomachs and cat games.

"I guess I'm done playing now," said Nick.

"Me too," Smoke agreed. He knocked the broom down, blocking one male weasel.

The weasels were slow to react, but they fought hard, and for ten minutes, it was difficult to see through cloud of flour dust. But in the end, their arrogance cost one male and the female weasel their lives. Nick and Smoke gave the wounded male a message for Rogo, and then let him limp up the flour slide to deliver it.

Smoke and Nick dragged the dead weasels up the slide to bury in the snow. When they were done, Smoke remembered their interrupted conversation.

"What did you say about a human seeing us—ya know, before we got into it with the weasels?" he asked.

"So you didn't see him?" said Nick.

"No. Tell me."

Nick looked up and down the street once. "Okay, but let's get back inside. I'm not picking up any scent of live weasel, but we don't know that one isn't getting reinforcements either."

"Fine, but try not to clobber me at the bottom this time," Smoke said as he dropped from sight. Nick followed him down the slide, and continued his story.

"Right after you went down the slide the second time, I heard a sound, and then, just like that, a human boy rounded the corner. He looked right at me, so I froze. And that seemed to work. He didn't come any closer. But then he talked to me. He called me something. And the way he said it…it was like we were best friends."

"I think the cold is affecting your brain," said Smoke.

"I mean it, Smoke, I've never heard anything like it. When he spoke to me, his eyes got bright, and his mouth broke into lots of happy teeth.

"So what?"

"So I answered him."

"You what?" Smoke jumped to his feet.

"Then the ice broke, I let go, and landed on top of you," Nick finished.

"I can't believe you let him see you! Let alone talked to him. And he knows where we are. You agreed to lay low until we figure this place out. What if he sends more weasels after us—or humans?"

"He won't. I know he won't."

"Right!" Snarled Smoke.

"And if you'd heard the—wanting—in his voice, you'd have talked to him too," Nick growled.

"For all we know, he 'wanted' you for dinner," Smoke snapped back. The grey cat's voice dropped as if he were talking to himself. "Every time I think you've changed, you do something reckless."

"It's going to be okay, Smoke—and you should watch what you're saying."

"No! I've had it, Nick. You just keep putting yourself first. And that puts Rose in danger."

Nick felt stung. So his friends thought he was selfish and dangerous?

"I saved Rose, remember, Smoke? Neither of you would be here without me."

Smoke crouched into an aggressive position. "Rose led us here, Nick, not you."

Nick matched Smoke's aggressive position. He was willing

to chalk Smoke's barb up to too many days of stress and fear. He knew Smoke had never before fought for his life on a daily basis. But Nick wanted to know where he stood.

"So now that we're here, you want to get rid of me? I thought you were my friend."

"I am your friend. But we don't even know what's going on in this village, and you called attention to us. If you want to tip off the humans, I can't stop you. But I can put some distance between you and Rose and me."

Smoke and Nick stared at each other for several heartbeats. Smoke sat up. "I'm going to try to find out more about the village—on my own," he said.

"You don't see me stopping you." Nick's voice was dead calm.

Smoke turned, crossed the room and clawed his way up the bakery slide. Nick stared at the empty slide, remembering the longing he'd heard in the boy's voice. "I know he won't tell," Nick said to the empty room, "I know he won't."

CHAPTER THIRTY-SEVEN

The City of Singing Stones

Mark remained beside the bakery ramp. After two self-inflicted pinches, he still had no idea whether he'd seen Shift, or a real cat. He kept hoping the animal would show itself again, and after a cold wait, he tested the flour slide to see if he could sneak into the bakery. The wooden ramp creaked at the first touch of his boot. Mark jumped back, well aware that he was an eleven-year-old, trying to get into Mr. and Mrs. Dresden's bakery in the middle of the night. With suspicions and tempers running high in the village, his story suddenly felt weak. Frustrated, he headed for the hill that would take him home.

If he'd seen a real cat, how long had it been in the village? And why hadn't he seen it before? Was the cat the one stealing food and doing all the damage? Mark's heart sank. If the animal he'd seen wasn't Shift, then it could be the "Christmas Villain." But the cat hadn't acted very wily or afraid—and what cat ate Christmas cookies?

Maybe there'd been no cat and he was just crazy. Mark stopped walking.

Then he started up again. If people found out a stray cat was loose, guilty or not, it would bear the brunt of the anger that had built up in the village. The families worked hard, and all year they looked forward to the holidays and celebrating Christmas. But this year, nearly every cottage had lost food or gifts, or had something special destroyed. He'd never seen the adults so ill-tempered. But until he had proof of guilt, Mark stood firmly on the cat's side.

He'd climbed the hill at a fast pace. At the front door, he paused to slow his loud breathing. He opened the door, stepped inside and sat to remove his boots. On stocking feet, he tiptoed to the door of his parents' bedroom to check on his mother.

"Mark, is that you? You okay?"

"I'm fine, Mom, I'm just goin' to bed."

"G'night, honey. Sweet dreams."

"Night, Mom."

Up in his loft, Mark wrestled between his exhaustion and his vow to stop dreaming. He looked at his soft bed. He'd just get warm under the covers and read something. He didn't have to go to sleep. He climbed beneath his thick comforter, wondering if Shift knew about the cat hiding in the bakery.

Then he remembered: He didn't know if there was a real cat. He wouldn't have a chance to ask Shift, because he wasn't supposed to dream. And he couldn't be completely sure he wasn't already dreaming—or crazy. Mark groaned and opened his book.

He was asleep in seconds.

·§·

Mark and Shift sat side by side on a tree branch, thirty feet above the ground.

"It's a good thing we brought the rope," said Mark. The smooth trunk had been a challenge to climb, but their limb provided a terrific view of the vast hilltop city before them. Dozens of people in feathered costumes formed a circle on a broad mesa. A massive, carved stone stood in the center of the circle.

Mark shifted position to remove the crossbow hanging from his shoulder. "How did you know about this place?" he asked.

"The City of Singing Stones is legendary. I'm surprised you've never heard of it," teased Shift, a wide grin on his leopard face.

Mark grinned back. "Who'd have guessed a whole city was hidden up here?" The people on the mesa were swaying in unison. "Do you know what they're doing?"

"They're about to raise that capstone into place atop the citadel."

"So the ropes and pulleys are hidden under those feathers?"

"They don't use—listen, they've started. Watch the capstone."

Mark heard a low hum, like the deep drone of a beehive. Moments later, the sound swelled, gathering strength to become a chant. The capstone quivered, and then lifted inches off the ground.

Mark's jaw dropped. "They're raising that giant stone with sound?"

"Yep. Get the crossbow ready."

"What? Why?"

"Just in case," said Shift.

"Okay. It's loaded, but what am I—"

The chanting voices grew louder. Every singer focused on the capstone, and it rose into the air at a steady rate. One moment the stone hung directly across from Mark and Shift's perch. With the next surge of voices, it hovered higher than their tree.

Mark's body vibrated. "It feels like the mountains are singing."

"They are. And the plants and animals, and the sky too," Shift answered, his eyes locked on the scene. "Legend also says there is one who refuses to join their song. The citadel would be a defense against him, and he—"

Mark and Shift saw them at the same instant: Eighteen black stallions racing across the sky toward the hilltop city, flames shooting from their mouths. They pulled a chariot of carved onyx rimmed with gold that glinted in the sun. A gladiator, red hair and beard streaming in the wind, lashed the horses to fury. He looked as big as an oak tree, and equally strong.

People on the mesa cried out. The circle of chanters continued to sing, but the capstone halted mid-air. The charioteer howled a thunderous war cry. Mark wanted to cover his ears, but reached out to grab Shift instead. Their tree shuddered in the shock-wave that rolled over them.

The chariot circled above the chanters, the gladiator dropping the reins to lift a boulder the size of a mill wheel overhead. He hurled the boulder at the circle. The missile skidded across the hilltop and through the circle, crushing feathered figures. In slow motion, the capstone began to fall to Earth. When it crashed, many more would die.

"The crossbow!" Shift yelled. "It's their only chance!"

"I'm too far away!"

"I can change that," Shift answered, stepping to the end of their branch.

"What are you doing?" Mark cried.

Shift began to warble a song different than any he'd sung before, a dark whisper of inevitable doom. The charioteer's head came up, listening. A heartbeat later, his eyes turned to Shift like a hawk finding its prey. The gladiator aimed his steeds for their treetop.

Shift ceased his song, but remained where he was, facing the charging chariot. "He hasn't seen you, you're hidden by the leaves. You'll only get one shot. But you can do it." Shift stood his ground, eyes welded to the charioteer's.

Mark's hands trembled as he aimed the weapon. He waited until he heard the crackle of flames from the horses' mouths. The charioteer again dropped the reins to raise a deadly boulder, his eyes riveted on Shift.

Mark let his arrow fly. The missile struck the giant's neck, but he didn't falter. He turned eyes red with rage on Mark and aimed the boulder again. And without a sound, he slumped forward, the stone falling from his dead hands. The frenzied horses veered in a sharp turn to race back in the direction they'd come, the unbalanced chariot tipping to one side. The body of the dead colossus fell into the deep chasm below.

Shift turned his attention to the descending capstone. He warbled new notes, and the remaining figures on the mesa added their voices to his. The capstone climbed back into the sky. Minutes later it sat in place atop the citadel.

The people of the singing stones carried Mark and Shift on their shoulders to seats of honor.

Mark awoke with the roar of their cheers echoing in his ears.

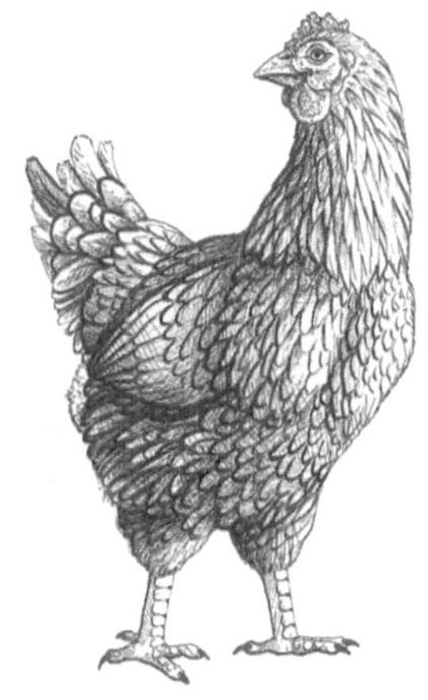

CHAPTER THIRTY-EIGHT

Redfeather

At the top of the bakery slide, Smoke turned right and headed for his original destination. From the hillside last night, he'd noticed fenced pasturelands and large buildings across the river. Now he wanted to talk with Dreamhaven's farm animals. Like cats, they lived closely with humans and often had good information.

As he walked, he paid attention to the scents and sounds on the wind, especially with a human boy and weasels on the prowl. But the grey cat couldn't completely ignore his thoughts. He hadn't meant to snap at Nick, but now that he had, Smoke realized he'd been angry for days—at Bart, at Nick. And at Rose when she wouldn't leave Nick behind. They were still in danger and homeless.

But he had to admit, Rose had been right about Nick being alive, and Smoke was glad.

He stepped onto the stone bridge spanning the river. He shivered in the chill mountain breeze that flowed down the valley and through the village. But the fresh air swept away some of the bitterness of the journey, their battles with the weasels and his argument with Nick. Suspended over the frozen water, Smoke relaxed. He stood mid-span looking down at the moonlit ribbon stretching away beneath him.

The river felt like a beckoning road. The night breeze agreed, blowing through the bridge railings to make exotic music. Smoke whispered back. "I hear you, river, and if I get the chance, maybe someday I'll follow you from here to the sea. But right now, I have to explore the village." With a final salute to the gleaming pathway, Smoke trotted to the end of the bridge and out onto the far riverbank.

Ten minutes later, Smoke approached two enormous stone pillars flanking a gate of blackest iron. Though he typically ignored gates, he found this one worth notice. In the lower right corner, the metalwork held the face of a woman, her long braid of hair piled beneath her head. Smoke wondered how anyone could make iron look so soft.

The woman's lips were blowing on a dandelion, the metallic seeds scattering across the gate. Smoke saw that on the other arm of the gate, the seeds had become leaping fish and geese flying in a "v." At the far edge, a pair of horses raced the wind beneath a crescent moon and stars.

Smoke knew that the artist who'd made this gate had been

places and seen things. And Smoke wanted to see them too. He stepped through a gap in the artful ironwork.

The farmhouse beyond was larger than other homes in the village, and had the only window of colored glass he'd seen in Dreamhaven. He was surprised that several rooms were ablaze with candlelight at such a late hour. As he crept toward the house, Smoke saw a henhouse nestled beside the back porch. Without a sound, he placed an eye to a gap in the wooden henhouse wall.

Smoke counted a hen and six huge eggs, and from what he could see, that was too many for the small hen. She was brown with a single bright red tail feather, and as Smoke peeked through the crack, the chicken stood up atop the straw nest.

"I just don't know how much longer I can do this," sighed the bird, as she moved to another section of the nest. Her shift left three oversized eggs uncovered. A few moments later, Smoke watched the weary hen shift again. He could see that some of the eggs were always left cold and unprotected, no matter how hard the mother hen tried to cover them.

The breeze shifted and Smoke caught a whiff of weasels. He wasn't the only one interested in this farm. From her slow movements and drooping head, Smoke could tell that the bird was exhausted, and might fall asleep. If she did, he knew the weasels would make a fast meal of the little hen and her six brown eggs.

"I think I can help you," Smoke whispered through the gap in the wooden wall.

The hen jumped in surprise. She looked around to find the voice. "Where are you? Who are you? And…and how can you help me?"

"If you let me share your henhouse tonight, and tell me about the village and the owner of this farm, I'll warm your whole nest," answered Smoke. "That way you can rest without having to worry that any of your eggs will suffer from the cold or… anything else."

"You'd do that?" asked the bird. "Nothing would be more wonderful," she said to herself. She turned toward the door. "But how do I know you aren't a weasel, or worse? You'll have to let me see you face-to-face before I agree."

"Okay," said Smoke, "but don't forget, I've promised I won't harm you or your eggs, so don't be afraid when I show myself." He stepped into the hen house and sat down just inside the door.

"Why you're a ca, ca, ca—a CAT!" clucked the hen in alarm, flapping her wings at the edge of her nest. "Get out, get out. Leave us alone or I'll—" her red tail feather flicked in agitation.

Smoke stood his ground and spoke in a low calm voice. "I'm not your enemy. But the weasels are. And they're nearby."

The hen stepped back as if she'd been struck. Her head drooped. "How can I possibly trust you? How do I know you won't pounce on me at the first chance?"

"Well, I've given you my promise," said Smoke, "and I bet that's more than you've gotten from those weasels. And I've already had plenty of time to pounce, but I haven't."

The hen sat quiet, thinking. She stood up to move. "Oh, those dreadful misfits," she said. "They can't get through my door when it's closed, but they've come by for the last three nights making such a racket with their grumbling and threatening the whole night long. They've been up to no good, and I'm positive they're the reason Monsieur Marveilleux forgot to close the door to my henhouse tonight."

Smoke sensed that the mother hen wanted to talk. "Tell me what's happened," he urged.

The petite chicken was more than willing to chat about her

troubles. "Alright. I'll tell you, as long as you promise to stay right where you are until I'm finished."

"I promise. And I'm Smoke, by the way."

"Nice to meet you, Smoke—I think. I'm Redfeather." The hen settled on her eggs, and began her tale.

"Monsieur Marveilleux, the world famous artist who owns this farm, hasn't slept a wink for the last three nights."

"Why not?" asked Smoke, who settled to the floor with Redfeather's nod of permission.

"He's been searching day and night for his ice cream carving tools. They're unique in all the world, and M. Marveilleux brought them from Paris when he moved to Dreamhaven." The mother hen paused to sigh over the lost tools. With one black eye on Smoke, she moved to a new location atop her bulging nest.

"Of course without the special tools, there will be no Fabulous Frozen Fantasma, and—"

"What's a Fab…?" but Smoke, couldn't wrap his lips around the unfamiliar words.

"What is it? You mean you don't know about The Fabulous Frozen Fantasma? Dear, oh dear, oh dear me," clucked the hen in dismay at Smoke's misfortune. "Well!" Redfeather said with surprising energy, "The Fabulous Frozen Fantasma is a work of art, a tribute to inspiring dreams, and a delicious dessert. You see, the FFF is a twelve-foot tall by ten-foot wide ice cream sculpture.

"If your front gate is anything like what he carves in ice cream, I bet that's one amazing dessert," said Smoke.

"Oh, it is, indeed," enthused Redfeather. "But you haven't heard the best part yet. Each December one lucky person in

Dreamhaven has a wonderful experience. They are gifted with the Christmas Vision. Right here in the village, they dream of something unique, something no one has ever seen before. Then M. Marveilleux recreates that dream in perfect detail—out of ice cream. The Fabulous Frozen Fantasma is delicious, but it also brings good luck to the dreamer and to Dreamhaven."

The petite hen closed her eyes and continued in a distant voice. "Last year there was the mermaid playing a cello, and the year before, a prince with the wings of a griffin. But my favorite was the proud rooster wearing a Christmas medal on his chest and a crown of fireflies atop his red comb. He looked so gallant."

Lost in her memories, the hen sighed, but her eyes sprang open again as she remembered her feline guest. "But this December, no one has had the Christmas Vision yet, and M.M. is running out of time. Between the missing tools and the missing dream, it's a big mess."

"When is the Fabulous Frozen Fan-tas-ma unveiled?" Smoke asked, trying out the dessert's full title.

"Why, Christmas Eve, of course. It's always a beautiful, balmy night in Dreamhaven—has been since the time of Clavier." Redfeather moved to another section of her oversized nest.

"That's in two days," noted Smoke.

"And that's why M. Marveilleux has been tearing the house apart looking for his tools," said the hen warming to her polite listener. "But I'll bet you those weasels carried them off out of pure spite. They showed up right about the time the tools went missing."

"With all that dessert and good luck on the line, I'd think the whole village would be out looking for them."

"Oh no! It's a secret. Right now only M. Marveilleux, Mr. Draper, the ice cream maker, and Mayor Umworth know that no

one has had the Christmas Vision. But that can't last much longer. Not now that the Duchess of Sazore has arrived in Dreamhaven."

Smoke cocked his head in question. Redfeather perked up,
quite happy to enlighten him.

"The Duchess has come to unveil the Fabulous Frozen
Fantasma this year, and..." Redfeather leaned toward Smoke "...
if rumors about the Duchess are true, she plans to devour the entire FFF herself." Redfeather's tone was heavy with disapproval.
"The Duchess has brought her whole family to gobble—I mean,
to taste our masterpiece and..."

CHAPTER THIRTY-NINE

The Duchess, 6 Spoons & 3 Medals

Redfeather was right. The well-rounded Duchess had arrived in Dreamhaven that afternoon along with the Duke, their four children, one valet, eleven ladies in waiting, nine coachmen and the Duchess' personal maid, Fifi.

Her royalness had also arrived with a small, gem-encrusted chest. Inside lay six very large silver spoons especially created to eat the fabulous dessert. There were also three silver medals wrapped in sumptuous red silk, the highest honor of Sazore. One medal was for M. Marveilleux, one for Mr. Draper, the ice cream maker, and the last would go to Dreamhaven's mayor, James Jasper Umworth. The Duchess would bestow the medals just before she ceremoniously unveiled the Fabulous Frozen Fantasma on Christmas Eve.

In her room at the Dreamhaven Inn, the Duchess sat comfortably with an enormous cup of Sazoreberry tea. But her slippered foot tapped with impatience. She wanted Fifi to finish unpacking the trunks and leave the room as soon as possible, because the Duchess very much wanted to take a nap.

Her nap was the key to the Duchess' secret plan: In addition to unveiling and nibbling at the Fabulous Frozen Fantasma, the Duchess intended to dream this year's Christmas Vision—and get all the attention and good fortune that went along with it. The misguided villagers might think they'd had the winning dream, but they were sadly mistaken. She knew hers would be the only one worth carving in ice cream. And she was prepared to tell everyone so.

As the Duchess sipped her tea at the inn, Mr. Draper stood in the Dreamhaven Dessert Shop, his white hair ruffled with worry. Without a Christmas Vision and M. Marveilleux's ice cream carving tools, there would be no Fabulous Frozen Fantasma. Mr. Draper took his responsibility very seriously. He wanted to provide the perfect ingredients for Dreamhaven's good fortune. He painstakingly prepared his ice cream according to a secret recipe handed down through generations of Drapers.

But despite his best efforts, this could be Dreamhaven's first Christmas Eve without the legendary dessert.

The distraught man imagined the scene on Christmas Eve. Instead of sampling a mouthwatering spoonful of sweet luck from a twelve-foot masterpiece of gleaming ice cream, villagers and visitors alike would sigh with disappointment as they scooped their ice cream from a boring bowl. Mr. Draper had been as careful as ever concocting this batch, and the ice cream might still taste delicious. But no one would notice.

What would that mean for Dreamhaven? What would the Duchess do?" She was rumored to have a bad temper. "This is not good. Not good at all," Mr. Draper said aloud in his empty shop. "We need a plan." He hung the "Closed" sign on the door, and went in search of Mayor Umworth.

·§·

"…and so I'm afraid, dear Duchess, that despite our careful planning, without the tools there is no certainty there will be a Fabulous Frozen Fantasma for you to unveil," Mayor Umworth finished.

"Well!" the Duchess said crisply. She paced the full length of her spacious, velvet-draped suite, picking up speed with every turn. Her skirts whirled around her ankles like a small tornado. "Well!" the Duchess repeated even more crisply and quite a bit louder.

Mayor Umworth winced.

Smiling only on the inside, the Duchess felt delighted. A delay meant more time to have her special dream. She took two more silent spins through the room to devise her plan. Then she came to a stop in front of the two men, pulling herself up to her full, if modest height.

"Do you mean to say that I've traveled all this way, at considerable personal expense and vast inconvenience to my royal person, and now there's not going be a dessert?"

"Oh, there absolutely will be a dessert, Duchess. We'll still serve Mr. Draper's delicious ice cream in bowls, and…" the Mayor trailed off at the sight of the Duchess's stormy face.

"So, let me make sure I understand," began the Duchess in a voice dripping with disdain. "Instead of pulling the silken ribbon to reveal a twelve-by-ten-foot, world famous work of art, I, the Duchess of Sazore, will be pulling a dowdy napkin from a common bowl sitting atop a checkered tablecloth?"

"Oh, no, of course not, dear Duchess," answered the Mayor. "I'm sure the napkins will be arranged in alternating red and green, and the tablecloth will be a lovely solid, Christmassy color."

Mr. Draper's head sunk to his chest at Mayor Umworth's words.

The Duchess paused only long enough to glare at the Mayor until he turned a shade of red inappropriate for Christmas—or any other self-respecting holiday. She spoke in a voice hard as iron.

"In that case, I shall have to leave Dreamhaven this very instant and take with me the Duke, our four children, the valet, eleven ladies in waiting, the nine coachmen, six very large spoons and three silver medals wrapped in red silk. Fifi!" Bellowed the Duchess. "Commence packing!"

As the maid circled the room gathering up the same shoes, hats and jewelry she'd just unpacked, Mr. Draper nudged Mayor Umworth with a pleading look.

"Madame Duchess," began the Mayor, "won't you do us a great honor and stay a bit longer? We're still very hopeful that M. Marveilleux will have everything he needs in time."

The Duchess remained silent, turning the full force of her withering, royal gaze on the Mayor. Her right foot tapped the carpet as she folded her chubby arms in front of her generous bosom.

"Uh, shall we say a full week…at no charge?" the Mayor continued. The tapping foot picked up speed. "And," he continued, desperation creeping into his voice, "Mr. Draper has a surprise he's been saving for you." Mayor Umworth pushed the stunned ice cream-maker closer to the fuming Duchess.

"The-May-or-is-of-course-speaking-of…" Mr. Draper said, stretching out each word for all it was worth, "…of 'Duchess Delight,'" he offered in a final rush of words. "Yes. That's it! I've been inspired by your royal presence to name my newest ice cream flavor after your royalty. It's very rich and has a…a very, well-rounded flavor—"

"That's the one, Draper," the Mayor broke in, mopping his brow while nodding up and down in enthusiasm. "Bound to be your most popular flavor yet."

The Duchess smiled. "'Duchess Delight'," she savored aloud. "Oh, yes, that will do very nicely. Yet again, I've inspired the artiste to reach ever higher, far beyond his own imagination." Only after a long pause in which she appeared to consider the offer, did the Duchess allow herself to be persuaded.

"Fifi!"

The two visible bits of Fifi, her legs and the starched points of her white cap, came to an abrupt stop, smothered beneath an armload of the Duchess' oversized dresses. The petite maid curtsied toward the Duchess.

"Fifi, unpack the bags. We're staying. And do stop racing around. I want to take a nap. Immediately!"

CHAPTER FORTY

Smoked Weasels

In the henhouse, Redfeather's conversation switched from imitations of the Duchess, to serious issues at hand. "I wouldn't put it past those wicked weasels to steal the tools just to ruin our Christmas."

"I don't think there's much I can do about the missing tools tonight," said Smoke, "but I might be able to solve your weasel problem—if you let me."

The silence in the henhouse stretched into minutes. Smoke had not moved from his original spot by the door, and now he sat silent and patient. Rose had taught him that sometimes the very best thing to do was to wait.

Finally, the little hen shook herself, sending a soundless ripple from her brown head to the tip of her red tail feather. "If you get rid of the weasels outside, I'll trust you with my eggs—and my life" she declared with solemn dignity. "Then you can stay here the rest of the night, and ask me whatever you want. But only after I've had a nap, mind you."

Smoke nodded. "I'm glad you're going to let me help you, Redfeather. Now I need to figure out exactly how I'll do it."

Smoke looked over the henhouse. There wasn't much to it except wooden walls and a door with two hinges at the top. The door propped up on a stick inside the henhouse, and swung down to close. M. Marveilleux normally locked it from the outside until morning.

Five minutes later, Smoke had a plan to foil the weasels. His idea was simple. And it should work. But he knew the hardest part would be convincing Redfeather to play her part. The grey cat lowered his voice to a whisper.

"Okay, I know this is going to sound like a trick, but I promise you it's the best way for us to get rid of the weasels. You'll have to trust me, Redfeather." When the hen only eyed him without answering, Smoke took a breath, and went on. "I need you to close your eyes and pretend you've fallen asleep."

The hen's face filled with anger. "WHAAAAT?" she squawked. "And I trusted you…you unfeeling…feline." Redfeather puffed herself up for a loud fit of squawking to summon M. Marveilleux.

"No, wait!" Smoke urged. "Just hear me out. If you don't like the plan, I promise I'll leave."

Redfeather let out most of her air.

"You act like you're asleep. I cover myself with straw and

crouch out of sight just inside the opening. The straw should cover my scent enough for the weasels to think I've left. When they start to come through the door, I'll shove aside the stick, and the door will swing right at 'em. It's probably only enough to give them a good scare, but I bet they won't stick around. That's it. That's my plan. But I think it'll do the trick."

Redfeather started to puff up again, and Smoke realized his poor choice of words.

"No, that's not what I meant," Smoke whispered. "It is a trick, but only on the weasels. Honest." When Redfeather said nothing for several minutes, Smoke stood up and turned to leave the henhouse.

"You'd have to be awful fast to make it work," Redfeather said to Smoke's back.

Smoke stopped, turning his head to look at the hen. "If I weren't, why did you make me stay over here?"

Redfeather nodded her head, accepting the plan. Smoke nodded back, hoping that at least his smile looked full of confidence. He burrowed into the straw beside the door. With Smoke hidden, Redfeather settled into the middle of her nest, where she was most visible through the open doorway. She closed her eyes, but they sprang back open. Smoke kept watch on the henhouse doorway. Finally, Redfeather closed her eyes, kept them closed, and worked to breathe in an easy, sleep-like rhythm.

Outside, two weasels had been napping during their henhouse stakeout. The tan and white weasel woke from his nap and nudged his dozing partner. "Listen, they've stopped talking," Patch said.

"Finally!" said Benny. I thought they'd never stop their yapping." He looked through the henhouse door. "Yeah, she's nodded off. I don't see who she was talking to. Where'd they go? Why wouldn't we have seen someone leave?"

"I don't see anyone. Maybe she's just crazy."

"What if it's one of the cats? You know how sneaky cats are."

"If it was a cat, he probably slinked off since he couldn't talk a chicken into becoming his dinner. Besides, if he's still around, he'll have to take on the two of us. C'mon, now that the hen's asleep, let's make sure she gets a nice loooong nap."

"All right, let's bring home the meat."

The weasels ran toward the henhouse, and paused at the foot of the slatted, wooden ramp leading to the opening. They looked from the sleeping hen to each other, and then with lethal certainty, they dashed side-by-side up the ramp.

·§·

The moment the weasels' front paws reached the threshold, Smoke ran at the stick propping the heavy henhouse door open. As he hit the stick, he flattened himself against the wooden floor.

The hinged door swung over him to slam into the faces of both weasels. The tan and white weasel was knocked to the ground. The other lay unconscious atop the ramp. On her nest, Redfeather shivered with fear, but Smoke gave her a conspirator's grin. They remained still and silent, straining to hear what the weasels would do next.

"What was…what happened?" Muttered one weasel in a woozy whisper.

"It was the cat. Let's get outta here."

The weasel rolled over slowly, "Ooh, that hurts. Wait 'til Rogo hears about this! He'll eat that cat for breakfast."

"Yeah, let's go tell him how we lost a fat hen and six eggs to one lousy cat. He'll wanna hear all about how you…"

The angry voices faded as the weasels ran for the safety of their Dreamhaven hideout.

"We did it!" crowed Redfeather leaping to her feet at the edge of her nest.

"We did it," sighed Smoke, beaming at the mother hen in happy relief.

In her excitement, Redfeather had forgotten that she was now locked in her henhouse with a lightning fast feline. The next instant, she remembered. Smoke saw her collapse back onto her nest, her face etched with worry.

"I can't leave now," said Smoke, "but I'll sleep over here by the door for the rest of the night." He dropped to the wooden floor and closed his eyes.

A full minute passed. "No. No you won't," Redfeather said in a clear voice. Smoke opened his eyes to find her looking at him.

"You gave me your word and saved me and my eggs from certain death. Now it's my turn to keep our bargain." The petite mother hen stood up and stepped off her nest.

With great care, Smoke settled into place, stretching his body from one edge of the straw nest to the other. He wasn't touching the eggs, but his body's warmth rolled over all six love-ly brown eggs.

He and Redfeather dozed off.

A short time later, the new friends awoke to sounds in the bushes outside. They moved to peer through a knot in the wall of the henhouse. They could just make out lantern light in the bushes.

"Ah! Ah-ha-ha! I have found zee tools!" exclaimed a man's triumphant voice.

Smoke and Redfeather smiled at each other. They returned to

the nest to settle and go back to sleep, when Smoke said, "I can't wait to tell Rose and Nick about this."

"Who?" Redfeather yawned.

"My sister, Rose, and my best—" Smoke faltered, remembering his argument with Nick in the bakery. That didn't seem to matter so much now. "My best friend, Nick," he finished.

Dempsey

Rose looked up, shocked to see how far the stars had moved. Much of the night had already passed. "I'd much rather stay here with you, Clavier, but I should explore the village."

"I understand." Clavier bent low. Rose jumped from the tall woman's shoulder to the pedestal. She looked toward the village, and then turned back to her new friend.

Clavier smiled. "I've enjoyed our visit. I hope your reunion with Smoke and Nick is filled with good news. And, Rose, if there's something I can do, I will."

Rose took a deep breath, basking in Clavier's words. So much had happened since Bart had stuffed them in the sack and left them for dead. But Father Christmas's visit and Clavier's guidance had saved them.

Rose rubbed lovingly against Clavier's ankles. "Thank you—for everything. I'll remember all you've told me."

At the crest of the hill, Rose looked back. The beacon burned brightly, and moonlight once more kissed a bronze Clavier.

Rose wove her way through the deserted paths of Dreamhaven. She had no plan, but she was ready to learn more about the village. She followed the riverbank for a while, until she saw candlelight shining in a nearby cottage. She moved toward the light and stopped outside a modest home. Despite the wisdom of staying in the shadows, Rose couldn't resist sitting for a moment in the golden square of candlelight that fell from the cottage window.

"Mmmmmmm." As Rose inhaled the smell of warm parlor fire, her longing for Adele was almost overpowering. Rose would try to reach Adele in dream again as soon as they were safe. Maybe they could connect once she could rest and concentrate. But she didn't know if they'd ever be reunited.

And Rose wasn't sure she'd ever trust another human that much again.

She heard the murmur of a song in the house. The melody rose and fell, like a mountain stream idling down a slope, and the words were filled with dreamy thoughts, as light and untroubled as clouds.

·§·

"Go to sleep my little, Stephan…" Joycelyn could hear strain in her voice. The last few nights had been difficult. First, Joycelyn had discovered a gnawed cookie in a tympani drum. Then her husband, David, had found one of their Christmas ornaments and two pieces of Joycelyn's jewelry in the mouth of the tuba. If this was someone's practical joke, neither was laughing, because one-year old Stephan hadn't slept for the past two nights.

"Waaaaah! Weeaaaaaaah!" The baby in her arms cried, frustrated and unhappy. He wasn't sleeping, neither were his parents, and that definitely hadn't worked out well for David earlier in the evening.

He'd been hired to play at the banquet in honor of the Duchess of Sazore, accompanying Felicity, the Mayor's wife, in the debut of her first opera.

"I guess I nodded off at the piano during the long speeches," David explained to Joycelyn. "It was only for a moment, really. But my nose bumped the sheet music, and all the pages tumbled from the holder, scattering across the carpet."

"Oh, dear," Joycelyn said in sympathy. "What did you do then?"

"No one seemed to notice, so I sort of folded up, slid under the piano and crawled across the floor grabbing music."

Joycelyn had to hide a smile at the thought of her very tall husband trying to sink beneath the piano unseen.

"I'd just crawled back up onto the piano bench when Felicity announced, 'I will now perform my latest composition, *Father Christmas's Snowy Quiet.*' I launched into the first page of the music propped in front of me. But instead of Felicity's aria, it was the other piece I'd chosen for the evening, the one to amuse the children, *March of the Elephant Maidens.*"

"I know the one. It's very fun, and quite loud..." she trailed off as her husband winced. "What happened next?" she asked.

"The huge, booming notes hung in the air forever. At first the audience sat in shocked silence. Then one person giggled, and then another, until the room erupted in titters. No matter how hard they tried to stop their laughter—behind hands, beneath napkins, or by concentrating very hard on the white linen tablecloth—they giggled. Finally they were laughing out loud. It would die down, but a single glance could set the whole room off again."

Joycelyn started to giggle too. "I'm sorry. But it does sound like one of the best evenings Dreamhaven has had in awhile. A little fun is just what the village needs."

"Tell that to the Duchess. I apologized, but she denounced the event as 'a serious breakdown in manners.' Then she drew herself up into a tower of offended dignity, and stalked from the room. It was truly, horribly awful," David finished, his face buried in his hands.

Joycelyn kissed her husband on the cheek. "Don't worry anymore, she said softly. Tomorrow we'll apologize to Felicity again." We'll tell her about Stephan not sleeping, and with four sons, I'm sure she'll understand. And…we'll insist she sing on Christmas Eve instead. Think how much she'll enjoy that."

"I hope so," David croaked, too tired to say more.

Stephan had finally drifted off to sleep in Joycelyn's arms. "Right now," she continued, "we need to get to bed, and hope all of our sweet dreams return tonight." She tucked the baby into his bassinet by the fire, and led her husband to bed.

Just outside the musicians' door, the familiar scents and sounds of a home pulled hard on Rose. As if in a trance, the dreamdancer moved toward the cozy house. She'd reached the bottom step leading to the front door, when she saw a large dog step into sight only two yards away. Rose was downwind, and the hound hadn't seen her yet. But he had a clear view of the entire lane. If Rose ran, his long legs would close the gap between them far too fast.

She crouched down, crawled up the steps and backed up against the closed front door, doing her best to hide in a shadowy corner. She watched the floppy-eared hound, her heart racing. There was still a chance he'd go in another direction. But the wind shifted. The dog lifted his nose to the breeze, and headed straight for Rose. She'd have to run. She tensed to push off the cottage door.

"Whup! Bang!" Without any warning, Rose fell backward into the darkness of the house.

Her heart beat with terror, but her eyes quickly adjusted. She lay in a small snow porch. She understood in an instant that when she'd pushed back, the pet door had given way behind her, and then fallen back into place.

But the bloodhound also knew where she'd gone. "HOOOOOOOWWWWL!" He shoved his long muzzle through the flap, forcing Rose into a dark corner cluttered with shoes and boots. Her back arched in terror and her tail doubled in size. Rose tried to escape the footwear, but she was trapped inches from the straining dog's jaws. And his barks would alert the humans. The dog used his hind legs to push himself further through the small pet door.

"Wa-wa-waaaah!"

A woman ran from the bedroom to gather the baby into her arms. A man stumped toward the door holding a small candle. Rose was hidden in the shadows of hanging coats and piled shoes, but the light fell on the hound.

"Quiet, Dempsey! Bad dog!" The man's voice was loud in the small space. "What's wrong with you? Go home."

The dog withdrew his muzzle with slow reluctance. He sat outside gazing up at the man through the window, his face mournful with disbelief. "Go on, now. Go... no, I mean it, Demps, go home now...that's a boy. Good dog." The man waited inside the door until the jangle of Dempsey's collar died away.

The woman had managed to calm the baby and tuck him back into his cradle. The bleary-eyed parents returned to the bedroom, and Rose shivered among the shoes.

Rose and Stephan

Rose lay still for many minutes. She felt exhausted, and she longed for Smoke and Nick. But it would be safest for all of them if she followed their plan and waited until their meeting time. And now that the hound was aware of her, she needed to find a hiding place in the house. She turned her attention to the living room, noticing its details for the first time.

Two well-worn chairs faced the fireplace, and a grand piano filled the right side of the room. The Christmas tree on the left stood just a bit taller than the mantel. Beside the tree, she saw a wicker cradle on rocker feet, where a white blanket draped over the sides and pooled in folds on the dark carpet. With one last listen, Rose crept into the cozy room.

"Ba, ba, bada uh, uh, uhhhhhhh."

The dreamdancer heard the soft sounds from the cradle. As if she were a feather caught in an updraft, she leapt up onto the cradle's curved top, setting it gently swaying. At the sight of a cat just over his head, the baby's tiny hands and feet clapped together, and he smiled a bubbly welcome. To her own surprise, Rose wanted to climb into the cradle. She knew she couldn't stay there long, but he looked so welcoming and happy.

Once she'd curled up with the delighted child, she calmed down and thought about Smoke and Nick. She hadn't expected to miss the way Smoke's tail flipped in his sleep, or the accidental scrape of Nick's claw when he rolled over. Or when those two purred so loud they woke her. But she did. She purred now, knowing she'd see them the next evening.

Rose awoke from a deep sleep to a tug on the white blanket. "Hey, little one, did you kick the blanket?" She whispered with a yawn. But the child remained sound asleep. When she felt a second tug, Rose came wide-awake.

She peered down through the woven basketry to see three young weasels standing together on the blanket. Their glowing eyes were red and hard in the dark. And they were staring up at the cradle. Their noses were working, but they didn't seem to know Rose was there. She guessed the smell of baby and baby powder masked her scent. But once that wore off, the weasels would either flee or launch an attack.

From the looks of them, attack would be their first choice. And once they started to climb, their sharp claws would bring them up and into the cradle in seconds. Rose glanced over her shoulder. The baby was awake and watching her. At best, the weasels would run around and over him, and he'd be terrified. At worst they'd bite him. Their teeth were sharp, and even a tiny bite could make him sick.

He was just a baby.

Despite the fear rattling through her, Rose knew that this was one of the tests Clavier had described. The dreamdancer reached a decision. She would do her best to protect the child. She was outnumbered, but surprise remained on her side. Turning to him, she gave the baby's foot a comforting lick.

"I'm not going to let them near you," she promised silently.

Stephan giggled back at her, pumping hands and feet in happiness.

In one fluid movement, Rose leapt out and over the edge of the cradle, her legs spread like wings. The weasels looked up to see a cat diving straight for them, eyes flashing in fury, claws out ready to strike. They scrambled to escape the soft folds of the blanket.

"Don't even think of touching this baby," Rose hissed, driving the weasels toward the front door. She hoped her momentum and their shock would keep the weasels running right through the flap. And she dreaded what would happen if they turned to fight her. But the sight of a flying attack cat had been too much. The weasels ran at the flap as if it was made of butter. They were through it and gone in the blink of an eye.

Rose waited in the shadows to see if the noise of her attack or the fleeing weasels had awakened the baby's parents. But when no one stirred from the bedroom, she took up a sentry position beneath the cradle, the white blanket concealing her from view. She soon heard the child's deep, gentle snoring above her.

Rose felt surprising warmth for the little one, and she was grateful to know that Bart hadn't destroyed her faith in humans.

From her cozy retreat, Rose reached out for Adele in dream. And found her.

"Rose? You're alive?" said Adele. "I thought—when I couldn't find you in dream, I thought I'd lost you. I've missed you more than words can say. Is Smoke okay? And our blue friend too? Where are you?"

Adele's happiness was contagious, further soothing Rose's most recent terror. "We're okay. We're in a village high in the mountains."

"I don't know how you got there, but I'm so glad you're alive. I didn't think I'd ever feel this happy again. Are you sure you're okay?"

"We're safe, right now," said Rose.

"Bart's story of you running off didn't fool me for a minute. But then when he bragged about killing you, I believed him. I went into the kitchen, took off my wedding ring, and laid it on the table. Then I went back to my mother's. Tell me what really happened."

Rose described Bart's treachery, but she downplayed the worst hardships and the hopelessness they'd felt. Adele had already suffered enough for trusting her husband.

Then Adele told Rose about her mother's fall and her continuing frailty. As she listened, Rose grew more and more certain that Adele could not leave her mother to find them. And, worse, that three cats would be too much for Adele and her mother to care for, even if the cats traveled to them.

"We only arrived last night, but we're safe," Rose assured Adele, hiding her disappointment. "We've found plenty of food in the village, and now we're discovering…all Dreamhaven has to offer, and…"

As dawn peeked through the cottage windows, Rose left

Adele's dream with promises to return often. Awaking, Rose felt the hard truth in her heart. Adele needed to care for her mother, perhaps for years to come.

She, Smoke and Nick were on their own.

Too Close for Comfort

Nick paced the bakery floor long after Smoke departed. With no one left to fight, and no way to convince Smoke he was right about the boy, Nick knew he either had to bed down for the night, or burn off some energy. He leapt to the flour slide and clawed his way to the top. At street level, he looked up and down the lane, and then dropped to the snow. He was glad to be outside, but he'd have to keep moving to stay warm and he'd need a safe place to curl up.

Early in his travels Nick had discovered that humans with the least to share were often the most generous. He recalled

Germany. He'd huddled beneath two sweaters and a comforter in a drafty room lit by a single candle. Despite her own hunger, the pale teacher had fed him her week's ration of butter. He just needed to find the right person. Maybe he could track that boy and hide at his house. Then Nick remembered his argument with Smoke over the human. "Bad idea," he decided aloud. His stomach rumbled.

If he was going to stay in Dreamhaven, he definitely wanted to know where to get the best food in town. Everyone loved to eat, and the village had probably sprung up around a good cook, and grown from there. He'd head for the oldest buildings in the village. When Nick reached the magic shop, he headed west testing the wind often for the scent of threats and food he wouldn't have to chase down or fight.

"Dinga-dinga-ling." Despite the late hour, the door of a shop opened with the ring of a brass bell. A white-haired man stepped out, preparing to close up and go home. Nick froze in the shadows, watching.

"It's been a long day," the shop owner sighed to himself. "And if we're lucky enough to find the tools, I'll have another early start tomorrow." He stepped into the snowy lane, and paused for a moment, his hand on the open door.

"HOOOOOOOWWWWL!"

The man looked in the direction of the sound. Nick lost no time. He dashed for the open door.

It took only a moment for the man to recognize the hound's voice and shake his head at the mournful bay that broke the deep quiet. But that was long enough for Nick to enter the shop unseen. The man pulled the door firmly closed and turned the key in the lock. As the door swung into place, the moonlight revealed golden letters in flowing script:

The Dreamhaven Dessert Shop

Now that he was inside, Nick wasn't sure he'd find any cat food. But he was sure to find a safe place to sleep. Besides, there were so many new sights and smells he was content to roam around. A mountain of fresh, buttered popcorn stood in a tall glass case.

"That smells delicious," Nick said aloud, his voice filled with admiration. On the counter beside the popcorn, lay a very large knife, and a row of round glass jars with heavy glass lids. The jars were as tall as a small bucket, but not quite wide enough for a full-grown cat to jump into. Each held a different mystery, and even if Nick didn't know what the hand-lettered labels on the outside of the jars meant, he liked what he saw inside: There were chocolates in the shape of Father Christmas in the first, and thick slabs of fresh peanut brittle poking up at easy-to-reach angles in the next. The blue cat glided on to the third jar, and quickly moved in a wide arc away from it. The black licorice in the shape of spiders sent a shiver down his spine.

Next, a smaller jar stood full of tiny sticks, and even with the lid on, the tangy scent of mint reached out to tickle Nick's nose. On the counter sat a plate of honeycomb that smelled like the dark and secret places of bees. But Nick was sure it couldn't taste as delicious as the hive Rose had found. In the glass-fronted case, the top shelf was dedicated to painted tins in the shape of ships, pyramids and butterflies. The bottom shelf held caramel covered apples, resting on flattened, sticky tops.

Nick had seen and…mmmmm…smelled enough. Without a doubt, this man could cook. He wondered what the white-haired chef could whip up with fresh weasel meat.

But the best was still to come.

Following the sound of a gentle, but steady drip, Nick discovered a massive metal box where huge slabs of ice slowly melted into a drainpipe. Nick leapt to the glass top for a better look, and looked down into the upturned mouths of ten round tins.

Nick laughed. "Those colors are fantastic," he said to the empty shop.

Some tins sang in bright shades of pink, orange, yellow and green; the whites were laced with sticky chocolate stripes or chunky with hazelnuts and almonds; the creamy texture of chocolates dark and white sat side-by-side; and beside those stood deep stains of raspberry red and boysenberry blue. In an instant, Nick fell under the spell of those ten tins. Anything this pretty had to be good, he decided. "Which one shall I ask to try first? Maybe that stripey one…well, or maybe the green one…"

Nick was so busy making delicious decisions, that a good 30 seconds passed before his brain identified a new sound—chewing. His head came up, his ears alert for more information. He looked over his shoulder toward the noise coming from the front of the shop. His ice cream-induced rapture evaporated.

Two male weasels, one adult and a juvenile, stood upright beneath the popcorn case. They were staring at Nick. The older weasel casually chose another piece of popcorn from a display bowl and popped it into his mouth, crunching the buttered kernel between sharp front teeth.

Nick slowly turned around atop the ice cream case, and dropped to a crouch facing the weasels. On the outside he looked wary, but calm. Inside, his thoughts were racing almost as fast as his heart. Were there more weasels hiding in the shop? Why would they advertise themselves if there weren't? He could probably take the younger one, but the other guy looked pretty confident. Probably best to come out swingin'—and soon…

Nick took a deep, steadying breath. His mind made up, he tensed for a running leap across the ice cream case. Unfortunately, the glass beneath his paws was smooth, and for several seconds, his legs ran, but he went nowhere.

At the sound of his glassy scramble, the younger weasel climbed to the marble countertop. The adult weasel remained beneath the popcorn case. Nick had just managed to grip an edge and jump to the floor, when the big weasel spoke.

"Whoa, my friend. There's no need for you to ruffle that fine blue fur. I'm not here to fight. And I'm not going to run away either. No, I'm going to wait right here, because I want to chat with you."

Nick had already covered the twenty feet between he and the weasels. When he reached the floor in front of the marble counter, he stopped. He sat down, keeping the second weasel within his view, and his eyes level with the upright weasel on the floor. Nick's tail rose and fell in steady rhythm.

"Chat? Oh, sure, that makes sense. Last night you and your boogle buddies tried to kill us. So talking is the obvious next step. Why the sudden switch?"

"Last night, you took us by surprise." The weasel's voice rang deep, with a slow, relaxed cadence. "We thought the Dreamers had brought you in to drive us out. But now we realize that you cats and our boogle have a lot in common—when you think about it."

Nick's tension eased a notch, but he remained alert. Maybe Smoke was right about the weasels and the fights were all a misunderstanding. The weasels obviously knew lots about the village. It wouldn't hurt to play along for more information.

"How do you figure that?" Nick responded.

"It's not that hard to work out really. My name's Ralph, by the way, what's yours?"

Nick sat two feet from and directly opposite Ralph, who stretched his neck, first to the left and then to the right. It was such a lazy, slow motion, that Nick watched without concern.

"Forget the names. What makes you think we have anything in common?"

"Well, aren't you and your little cat family just trying to get by? Hmmm?" Ralph continued to stretch and twist his neck as if he were stiff and out of sorts. The weasel's eyes remained locked on Nick's.

"First, we're friends, not family, little or otherwise. Second, we don't attack strangers before we check them out. And third, we don't have a crazed, saliva-spitting maniac for a leader."

From the corner of his eye, Nick saw the weasel on the counter take a step. "You! Stay where I can see you," Nick's voice rang out.

Both the weasel on the counter and Ralph froze. Then Ralph went back to stretching his neck and upper body ever so slowly, his voice paced to the speed of thick honey.

"Oh yes, our leader, Rogo. You don't need to worry about him. He's more mouth than bite. And he's the one who sent us to reach out to you."

"'Reach out'? For what, my neck?" Nick felt suddenly tired, and he realized he'd dropped a little in his stance. He forced himself back into a fully upright position.

"Oh, that's funnnny. Who knew cats could be so entertaining? Yes, funnny…" The weasel moved a little more, twisting his upper body right and left.

Nick watched the weasel. He could go ahead and stretch, stiff.

ol' thing, just as long as he kept—Nick was surprised when he suddenly broke out in a full-blown yawn. Where had that come from? What had he been…oh, yeah, he just had to keep the old guy talkin'. Nick blinked hard, his eyes riveted on the undulating weasel.

Ralph grinned and then continued. "We want to propose an alliance between our boogle and you cats."

"Why…?" Nick yawned again, shaking himself to stay alert as Ralph swayed back and forth. "Why would we do that? Why would…?

Ralph dropped to all fours and took a step to the left of Nick. Nick responded instinctively, backing up a step closer to the counter.

"Because Dreamhaven is a nice old village, and there's plenty for all of us. We don't like the Dreamers. And by now, you must know that they don't like furry folk—of any kind."

"We don't, uh, we don't know that for sure…." Nick blinked hard, mesmerized by Ralph's swaying motions. "We…"

"Oh, but it's true. We've been coming into town for years to… get supplies. So we've had more than enough bad experiences with the Dreamers to prove my point."

Ralph took another step toward Nick, and though Nick felt strange and woozy, this time he held his ground.

Ralph sighed. "But, if you want to find out the hard way, that's okay. We can wait…"

Everything happened at once. Ralph ran toward Nick, and Nick backed up a step, crouching to fend off an attack, his tail whipping side to side.

"Now!" Ralph shouted.

Nick heard something heavy slide across the marble counter above him. With lightning reflexes, he hunched his body to the ground and rolled into the gap between the bottom of the counter and the floorboards.

"Thwannnnnnnnnng."

The massive fudge knife imbedded its sharp point in the wooden floor—along with one of Nick's whiskers. From his place beneath the counter, Nick stared at the shiny blade, quivering in the spot where he'd stood seconds before.

He saw all too clearly that he'd been a fool. Lulled by Ralph's hypnotic war dance, he'd stepped right into the trap the weasels had laid for him.

But now adrenaline fueled Nick's muscles. The blue cat leapt to the back edge of the marble counter, and landed behind the young weasel, who was leaning over the front edge to see what had happened. When the weasel turned, Nick was ready, his claws bared.

"Aaaaah. My eyes, I can't see!" the weasel screamed.

Nick rolled him off the counter onto Ralph.

"Get off, get offa me, you…" Ralph croaked, trapped beneath the weight of his writhing boogle mate. But Ralph's partner panicked. He lashed out with claws and teeth. "Stop! Stop clawing. It's me." Ralph screamed. "Stop biting! Get the cat!"

Nick watched the weasels roll across the wooden floor, now locked in fierce, deadly battle with each other. Minutes later, Ralph bled from several wounds, and the young weasel lay dead.

When Ralph looked up at him, Nick hissed, baring both rows of sharp teeth, but he did not attack. "Take this message back to headquarters," he spat. "Tell Rogo there isn't room for all of us in Dreamhaven."

Ralph limped backward and into the broom closet, never taking his eyes from the cat. A moment later, Nick heard the damaged weasel groan as he slipped beneath a loose floorboard.

"I guess weasel meat is on the menu here too," Nick said aloud. When he'd eaten his fill, he dragged the bones to the closet and dropped them down the hole. For dessert, he speared a single golden popcorn kernel on a claw and licked off all the butter. Cleaning the last buttery traces from his whiskers, Nick moved to a pile of clean rags in a nook between the popcorn case and the cotton candy display.

He settled down to sleep for the second time in Dreamhaven. And then he startled wide-awake. Last night—for the first time in his life—he'd gone to sleep without having his nightmare. He didn't remember crossing over to any of his other lives, but would he? He turned to ask Smoke. The grey cat wasn't there. And Nick didn't have any idea where Smoke was spending the night.

He also didn't know what would happen when he closed his eyes tonight. But he was ready to find out. "G'night, Smoke. G'night, Rose, wherever you are," Nick purred. And that was the last thing he remembered.

CHAPTER FORTY-FOUR

Meetings

In the post office the next morning, postmistress, Hil, handed the shredded remains of four letters to Angela Del'arte.

"I'm sorry, Angela, that's all that's left."

"But who would do such a thing? And why?" asked Angela.

Before Hil could say another word, angry voices in the street drew both women to the window. They saw Sam Cole and Joseph Worter locked in a shouting match. The two men had been inseparable friends for over fifty years.

"Where're you going, thief?" yelled Cole.

"What did you call me?" asked a stunned Worter.

"You heard me! I called you a thief. You've always been jealous of my gold pocket watch, and now you've stolen it."

"Of course I haven't."

"No one else has been in my house all week, and now it's gone. That makes you a thief—and a liar."

"Now you listen to me. I didn't steal your pocket watch or anything else. How dare you accuse me of such nonsense!"

In the narrow lane, villagers and visitors looked on, eyes wide, like unwilling witnesses to a train wreck.

Just then five-year-old Nathan came barreling around the corner of the post office at a run. He smacked into Mr. Worter and landed in the snow between the two red-faced men. Both stared down at him.

"I've gotta get Grandma's mail!" said Nathan, looking from one to another.

With a final glare at each other, the men helped Nathan to his feet, before storming off in opposite directions. Angela shivered as if a bitter wind had blown into the post office. Hil let out a long sigh, and stepped back behind the counter.

"That's the third argument I've seen in as many days," she said. "I think these nasty raiders stole that watch. They've been very clever at sneaking in and out of here without being seen. That makes me think it's the—"

Nathan slammed the door behind him. He stood eyeing the ripped letters in Angela's hand. "Grandma says we'll be lucky if there's anything left to open—or eat on Christmas Day," he blurted out. "I hope she's wrong."

Outside the Dreamhaven Town Hall, Mayor Umworth huddled with a dozen villagers. "I don't know who's responsible. But

I do know it's got to STOP," he said, pounding his gloved fist into his palm.

"Mayor, shouldn't you keep your voice down?" said a village man in a red scarf. "If visitors to town are still happy, we don't want them to know we're not."

The Mayor lowered his voice. "You're right, we don't need them to suspect anything is amiss. It'd damage our reputation and likely ruin their holidays. As if there aren't already enough other problems this Christmas."

"What could be worse than vandals, thieves, and losing our wonderful dreams?" asked a woman. "What problems, Mayor?"

"Nothing, nothing at all," he muttered, sorry he'd let his worries over the Fabulous Frozen Fantasma lead him into a blunder. "But I'm calling a town meeting tonight to come up with a plan to get to catch these culprits. We were dreaming just fine until their villainy began."

At 3 o'clock that afternoon, the town crier, a bear of a man with a voice to match, took up position in front of the post office to make an important announcement. But, as he opened his mouth to speak, he noticed that several visitors to Dreamhaven were listening. The Mayor had given him very clear instructions about that.

"If they hear talk of thieves or damaged presents, they might decide to leave Dreamhaven," Mayor Umworth had told him. "Or they might want to join the meeting, and we can't have that. So I'm counting on you to deliver the message without raising anyone's suspicions."

The town crier looked at the visitors, groaned once and snapped his jaw shut without uttering a word. Unfortunately for him, both villagers and guests were now showing even greater interest in him. He ran a nervous hand across his bald head, tapped long fingers on his black mustache, and at last re-opened his mouth to announce in a bold voice:

"All Dreamhaven residents are hereby asked to attend a meeting tonight at 7:00 in the Town Hall to discuss…important…Dreamhaven…stuff." The poor man stopped again, and despite the cold of December, sweat dripped from the tips of his mustache. "And…um…honored guests and visitors, you are heartily invited to stay away. Right. So all Dreamhaveners, you come and…everyone else please don't. I mean…please enjoy something else. Somewhere else. In fact anywhere else but in the Town Hall." His confusing message delivered, the town crier walked home to take a nap.

·§·

That evening, nearly every man, woman and child who lived in Dreamhaven arrived at the town hall by 7 o'clock.

"You know why we're here," said the Mayor. "What are we going to do about these malicious attackers? They're destroying our homes, our shops, and the reputation of our village is at stake. What are your suggestions?"

A tall villager sitting in the front row shot to his feet. "I don't have a suggestion, Mayor, but I'm warning whoever stole my Christmas ham, that they better return it tomorrow, or I'll make them wish they never saw that pig."

With that, angry voices broke out on all sides.

·§·

Meanwhile, in a corner of the Del'arte's magic shop, another meeting was in progress, with one scabby weasel doing all the talking. Rogo paced back and forth in a rage. Once he turned and bumped into the leg of one of the automatons. The mechanical man shifted forward, bringing his eyes even with Rogo's. The weasel leader leapt back startled. When he realized the automaton wasn't a threat, he kicked it on purpose, even harder.

"Look at us. We're reduced to hiding in a shop full of overgrown dolls!" Rogo ranted. The large weasel paused in his pacing to nibble on a festering scab. He wasn't the only one with reminders of skirmishes with the cats: Five weasels were dead with several more missing. And there were plenty of swollen paws, cuts and bruises among the survivors. But Rogo knew that he'd suffered the worst injury—the erosion of the boogle's confidence in him.

The remaining weasels stood or sat, shifting from paw to paw in silent discomfort. They'd learned the hard way that no response worked when Rogo was in one of his black moods.

"You heard Ralph's report," Rogo spat. "The cats are working for the villagers to push us out. And the villagers think we'll give up because they've set a pack of nasty cats on us. Well I won't stand for it," Rogo snarled, his tail swishing from side to side. "There has to be a smarter way to destroy the cats, and take revenge."

He looked around, hoping someone would dare to disagree. Instead, the candles in the shop window caught his eye. Rogo paused, and then he broke into an ugly smile. "Listen up everyone. I've got a plan. See those oil candles? I want you three to go out and lure those feeble-minded cats in here. And you four..."

Rose expected to be the first to arrive at the magic shop, but when she rounded the corner, Nick and Smoke were already there, deep in conversation.

"I'm sorry, Smoke," Nick said. "I'll do my best to be a better friend to both you and Rose."

"I'm sorry I got mad too, Nick. There is no excuse for my bad behavior."

"Smoke? Nick?" Rose called. Both cats trotted over, talking at once. Rose looked from one furry face to the other, laughing as she tried to hear all they were saying.

"…wait 'til you see the slide into the bakery…"

"…I know he saw me, but he didn't come after us…"

"…Redfeather lives across the bridge…"

"…so the weasels aren't pets…"

"…and Monsieur Marveilleux finally found his tools…"

"…but the knife just missed me…"

At Nick's words, Rose and Smoke turned to him, their eyes wide with shock. Nick looked from one worried face to the other.

"Look, I'm okay. Just one missing whisker—but no thanks to those rotten weasels." When neither of his friends spoke, he added, "And I found some great food."

Rose broke the silence. "I'm not sure I want to live there, no matter how good the food is." All three cats grinned.

"I vote we find a safe place to—" but Smoke never finished his sentence.

Up on the Roof

From the corner of his eye, Smoke saw movement by the large fir tree beside the magic shop. He froze, except for his head, which turned in a smooth swivel. A second later, Nick and Rose echoed his move. They were just in time to see a large, male weasel leap from the shadows to the tree trunk. The weasel seemed too intent on his climb to notice the cats, but they tensed, watching him move with ease to the lowest branches, until he was lost among the tree's snow-laden branches. Three sets of cat ears pricked to attention to trace the weasel's progress and his jump from the tree to the magic shop roof. Moments later, a second, and then a third weasel darted up the tree.

Nick ran to the tree, and dug his claws into the trunk, his strong legs propelling him up in fast bursts. Smoke climbed right behind him.

"So much for a quiet evening chat," sighed Rose. She sat alone in the snowy lane, watching the branches of the tree swish and bend with the male cats' upward clamber. "Seems like plenty of cats for the job, so I guess I'll just wait—" Rose paused, remembering the weasels' daring boldness. A moment later, she bounded to the tree and climbed to the roof.

Once up the tree, she saw weasels and cats disappearing over the farthest roof peak. Rose raced after them, but when she stood atop the peak, she found Nick and Smoke crouched down beside a dislodged roof tile.

"Where did the weasels go?" She asked

"Who cares? Look, Rose," Nick said, never taking his eyes from the hole in the roof.

Rose joined them, and soon all three cats were gazing spellbound into the shop. Below them the candles in the winter scene revealed a thick round rug, Robert Del'arte's workbench and so much more.

The Del'arte's shop was a well-organized collection of highly unusual objects that would have been intriguing any day of the year. But the humans had used the holidays as an excuse to drape thick garlands of bright tinsel from every available hook, rafter and curtain rod. The cats felt like they were peeking into the glittery bottle of an eccentric genie.

Three wide wooden shelves ran down one wall. Seated on the top shelf were two very life-like, human figures. With their bright porcelain eyes, open mouths and tilted heads, they seemed to have been interrupted mid-sentence. The first mechanical automaton was a shawl-draped woman with grey hair and deep brown eyes fixed on the crystal ball in her hands. The second figure was a mustachioed trumpet player in the scarlet uniform of a soldier.

"I like the dragons best," whispered Rose.

Two dragon automatons no bigger than a cat sat on the third shelf down, one green, one blue. Each clutched a faceted gem, and had impressive wings folded behind a plated neck. They gazed at the world with cunning, ancient eyes.

Nick's gaze was glued to the mechanical elephant. She faced the front door, wore a red bow and stood tall enough to look most ten year olds in the eye. Every few minutes she would lean back on her hind legs to raise her trunk in welcome. "How does she do that?" Nick asked aloud.

"She's somethin' else," Smoke agreed. "And that's a great snake," he added. The glistening serpent, wrapped three times around the nearest rafter, was as thick as a man's arm, and made of green leather covered in tiny sequins. Just beyond the snake, a wooden box hung from a golden rope, every inch glimmering with inlaid seashells and white stones in a pattern of trees and leaves.

But the best toy of all came out of nowhere in a blur of speed.

The lustrous black engine and red caboose of a model train appeared on a circular track suspended from the roof beams. The cats watched the train approach the far curve of track—and vanish. They stared at the spot dumbfounded. Seconds later, they heard a ghostly train whistle, and the engine reappeared, racing down the track toward them again.

"Oooooh, " Nick whispered.

"Oh, yes," agreed Smoke.

The two cats looked from the shiny engine to each other,

their tails twitching in perfect rhythm.

"Once in, our way out isn't clear," said Nick.

Smoke grinned and nodded once.

Rose remembered why she'd come to the roof and, uncomfortable, she sat up, scanning in each direction. "How could those weasels be so unaware of us? What if it's a trap?" she asked, turning back to Smoke and Nick.

"Too late now," said Smoke. "Nick's inside."

Then he dropped through the hole.

Illusions, Vanishings & Other Dangers

Rose followed him, the sides of the hole rubbing against her. She was well aware that the reverse jump was too high and too dangerous to use for an exit. But Nick and Smoke were already in motion, navigating wooden rafters that hung more than a dozen feet above the floor of the shop.

Rose knew where they were headed, but she was going to look for a way out. That meant exploring the rooms below. She walked to the end of the rafter and leaped to the third shelf on the wall. She stood between the two dragons, admiring them.

Glancing up, she saw Nick crouch, muscles tensed to jump, his eyes focused on the approaching smokestack of the magical train. She watched Smoke pad toward the other end of the roof beam to catch the train further down the track. He stepped over the wrapped coils of the snake and stretched forward to sniff the inlaid box.

"Pop!" The lid of the box flew open, and a mechanical orange tree began to "grow" at Smoke's face. He startled back, losing his footing.

"Mrrroowwwr," he yelled as he fell, desperately grabbing a loop of draped tinsel with his front paws. Rose and Nick watched in horror as the garland stretched tight and then sank into a "U" with Smoke's weight. They all heard the creak of straining nails, but the decoration held.

Smoke, dangling nine feet above the floor, looked up at Rose and Nick. "Close call," he laughed in relief.

Then one end of the garland gave way, swinging him through the shop at the shelves on the wall. Rose leapt for the safety of the carpet a second before Smoke plowed into the shelves, knocking all the automatons to the floor. Stunned, he disentangled himself from the garland, and dropped to the rug beside his sister. He did a full body shake, and tried to look casual.

Rose shook her head to let him know she knew better. She sniffed the air. "Do you smell that?"

"Weasel!" Smoke nodded. "And more than one."

They looked up at Nick, still perched above the train track.

"We're gonna' need some help down here," Smoke called.

"I'm on it. I'm on—" Timing his leap, Nick successfully dropped to the black locomotive as it rolled by. He sat astride the engine grinning as the train circled half the track. But moments later, his smile faded and his friends could see from the strain on his face that the train was moving much faster than he'd expected.

Smoke eyed the remaining track and the spot where the train always disappeared. The train was taking Nick closer every second. "Nick, you have to jump! Now!"

Nick launched into the air. From the floor, Rose and Smoke could tell he was aiming for the back of the elephant. Their muscles strained with his as he twisted in midair and stretched to his full length.

He might have landed safely on the back of the mechanical beast, but at the last moment she rose to her hind legs in greeting, slammed into Nick, and sent him flying, head over tail across the room. He sailed in a fast arc toward a tall cabinet covered with stars and moons.

"Oooof." When Nick hit the lacquered cabinet, the doors swung inward, and then, just as quickly, closed. A loud "click," locked Nick inside.

Rose and Smoke ran to the box.

"Nick!" Smoke called.

"Nick, are you alright?" Rose added.

Smoke stood on hind legs at the locked doors as Rose circled the tall cabinet. "How are we going to get him out?" he asked in a bleak voice.

"I've no idea," Rose answered, as both cats walked around the upright box, sniffing and searching for a clue how to open it. "But if the weasels come looking for a fight, we'll wish we were locked in there with him."

"No such luck. I'm out."

Rose and Smoke startled, tails bushy. Nick stood behind them.

"How did you—?" Smoke began.

"There's a trap door inside the box. The minute I hit the bottom, I rolled down onto a hidden ramp under the floor. It comes up over there, behind that curtain."

"Wow! A trap door," Smoke looked at the cabinet with longing.

"I'll be sore for days," Nick assured his friend.

At a skittering sound from the next room, all three cats froze. In unison they padded on silent paws to the opening between the work area and the front of the shop.

Rogo's Revenge

Rogo leaned casually on a carved deer in the miniature Dreamhaven village scene. The three weasels he'd sent to lure the cats up the tree and into the shop shifted nervously from foot to foot beside him. The trick had worked, and the cats were in the magic shop.

"We'll get rid of those filthy felines and teach the Dreamers a lesson at the same time," he boasted in a loud voice.

Ralph spoke up. "But there's no guarantee we'll escape!"

"I've already taken care of that," Rogo snarled. "That's why I'm the leader and you'll do what you're told." He stalked to the empty fireplace, stepping over the fresh logs stacked in front of it. "Go on. See for yourself," Rogo beckoned Ralph.

Rogo's discovery was a metal door the size of a piece of toast at the back of the fireplace. The humans used the door to remove ashes from the outside. The ash trap stood open, and Ralph poked his head through to see moonlit bushes and trees at the back of the shop where the rest of the boogle waited.

"Obviously, we can get out. But no cat can squeeze through," Rogo gloated in triumph. "I never took you for a coward, Ralph," he sneered.

Ralph said nothing, but as Rogo turned to watch the four unlucky weasels assigned to jump at the lit candles in the window, Ralph stepped through the ash door to freedom. The three nervous weasels darted through on his heels.

"Go on, you lazy lumps. Jump! Drag those candles down now!" Rogo screamed from the fireplace.

The candles were mounted just a nudge too high. And the "volunteers" weren't a hundred percent comfortable with Rogo's plan. They might not like the cats anymore than he did, but they weren't convinced getting rid of them was worth risking their lives in a burning building.

When all three cats stepped around the corner and into view, the weasels in the window panicked. One, then another, and finally a third ran from the window toward the fireplace and the escape hatch. But Rogo blocked their way, closing the door while he watched the remaining weasel leap. She hit the edge of the farthest oil candle, overturned it, and dodged the hot oil running down the window. Terrified by her success, the weasel raced to join her fleeing boogle mates.

The fiery oil flowed to the paper forest. A flame sprang up at the base of the nearest paper tree. Nick and Smoke charged toward the fire. The cats had no time to spare, and they ignored the bang on the door of the shop.

"The vase on the table!" Rose called out.

Smoke swerved for the workbench and a chipped glass vase. Nick ran to the miniature forest. He saw a second orange flame shoot up. He grabbed the burning forest in his mouth, tore it free and ran to the workbench.

Smoke hit the vase at a run. Flowers scattered, glass shattered, and water poured across the burning paper.

The flames sputtered and went out.

Smoke and Rose turned to check on Nick, but he whirled for the fireplace, and in one smooth leap, he stood within two feet of Rogo and the four remaining weasels. Rose and Smoke formed a tight "V" behind him. Rogo had forced the other weasels to stay so they could witness his triumphant revenge on the Dreamers and the cats. But now five weasels faced three angry cats.

"You mangy fools don't scare me." Rogo snarled in Nick's face.

"You've gone too far," Nick said in a quiet, dangerous voice.

"And you're an overgrown fur ball. I'm the leader of this boogle, and we own Dreamhaven," Rogo screeched in outrage. He sprang at Nick, teeth and claws fully extended. Pound for pound, Nick had all the advantage, but the enraged weasel was fearless. He aimed for Nick's eyes.

Nick didn't flinch as the mad-eyed weasel charged him. Instead he relaxed, encouraging Rogo's attack. Once the weasel committed, Nick slashed with razor sharp claws.

Fueled by anger, Rogo had underestimated Nick's reach. The blue cat raked a bloody track across the weasel's nose with a swipe that sent Rogo flying backward. Blinded by blood, Rogo recoiled for just long enough. The cats charged the other four weasels. Rogo lay pinned in place beneath battling cats and weasels. By the time he fought his way free, three weasels were dead, and the other two wheezed with pain.

And three bloodied cats, teeth bared, ears back, stood shoulder-to-shoulder, a solid line of uncompromising menace. The surviving weasels shoved the ash door open. One by one, they backed through the door, their black eyes never wavering from the cats. Once outside, they followed weasel tracks to the mail cart behind the post office where Ralph had taken the rest of the boogle to wait.

Inside the magic shop, Rogo stood alone, his back to the wall of the fireplace. His chest heaved up and down. Blood pulsed from his slashed nose to pool at his feet.

Nick's voice rang with lethal clarity. "You don't deserve it, but we'll give you a chance. Leave Dreamhaven for good, or die."

The cuckoo clock on the wall ticked away the minutes. Rogo stared hate at his enemies. The cats waited, still as stone. Finally, Rogo turned his back, and moved toward the ash door. His head had already passed out of sight, when he paused. The cats tensed, but Rogo's scarred backside and tail disappeared through the portal.

Nick, Smoke and Rose went to the window to watch. They saw the weasels gather at the edge of the mail cart. With slow, defiant steps, Rogo started toward the cart to collect the boogle. But when the post office door opened, he froze in the shadows.

The postman closed the door behind him, tucked his muffler tight and climbed into the driver's seat. "All right, Matilda, let's head for home." The man's voice was gentle, as he took the reins in hand. The mail cart moved toward the bridge.

"Get off the wagon, you fools," Rogo shrieked. "What are you waiting for?"

At Rogo's command, the youngest weasel moved to climb down. But Ralph blocked her way.

"What the…?" Rogo's splutter of rage died in his throat. His jaw sagged open, and his eyes bulged in disbelief.

The surviving weasels stared back at Rogo from the departing cart until they were swallowed by the dark.

Rogo stared at the empty wheel tracks for long minutes. Then he turned, and limped out of Dreamhaven.

The cats gathered in front of the fireplace.

"I bet those weasels don't leave that cart for the rest of the winter," laughed Smoke.

"Fast thinking to put out the fire," Nick complimented Rose. "And paws," he added, grinning at Smoke.

They licked their wounds, groomed and celebrated their survival. But they grew solemn when they saw the shattered automata, scorched Christmas scene, and puddled water around them.

"We can hide the bodies, but the humans can't miss this mess," said Smoke. "And the only way out for us is through the hole in the roof."

All eyes looked up, but the small hole was invisible high above them.

"I'm sure we could find a way back up there, but it's a long jump and a tight squeeze. If we miss or lose our hold, we risk a broken leg—or worse," said Nick. Rose and Smoke nodded agreement. They moved together, checking the rooms above the shop, but found no exit.

"Then there's no use hiding. We'll have to face the owners," said Rose.

Brother and sister walked on heavy paws toward the soft

cotton snow in Father Christmas's window scene. Minutes later, Smoke lay sound asleep, whiskers twitching, tail pulled close.

"I hope the humans see that this damage is better than a fire," Rose whispered to Nick, as they curled up beside Smoke.

"Yeah, but maybe if we sleep for a little while we'll think of something…" but Rose was already asleep and Nick drifted off before he could finish.

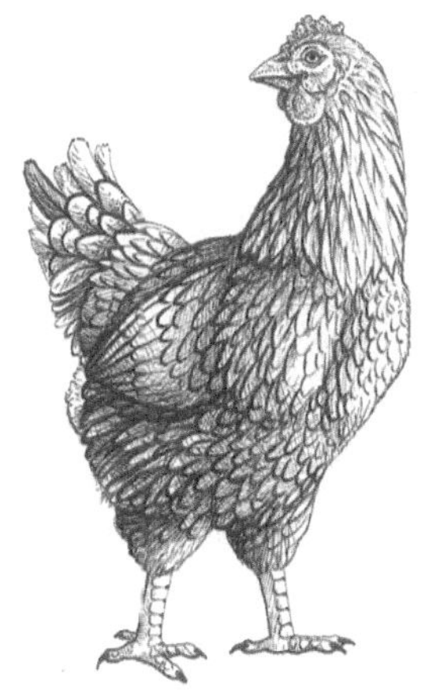

Discovered

Mark felt nervous going to the town meeting without his parents. But he wanted to hear if anyone mentioned a cat roaming the village. He had thought about the meeting carefully, and decided that the villagers were used to his father, Sean, being away in the forest for days at a time. No one would comment on his absence.

But his cheerful mother was another matter. He knew she would be missed, so Mark timed his arrival at the town hall late enough to be one of the last to slip inside. Only Angela Del'arte had a chance to ask about his mother.

Angela was a tall woman with a warm smile and large brown eyes. Younger than his mother, she and Minette had become close when Mark was only a baby. Angela insisted Mark call her by her first name. Now she touched Mark's sleeve and spoke in a soft voice with just enough Italian accent to hint at sunny places.

"Mark, how are you?"

"I'm fine. I'm okay, Angela, thanks. How are you?"

"Oh! Robert and I have been so distracted with orders for Christmas presents that I haven't seen your mother in nearly two weeks. But I'd hoped we'd get a chance to catch up during the meeting break this evening." Angela looked over the last villagers taking their seats. She turned back to Mark. "I don't see her. Where is she sitting?"

Mark didn't want to lie to anyone—especially not to his mother's best friend. He didn't know if his mom had talked to Angela about their…problems. From the gifts of fresh bread and soups Angela sometimes brought by, he suspected she knew something. But he didn't think she could know how bad things had become in recent weeks. Or that his father was gone.

"She isn't here, Angela. She…isn't feeling herself tonight," Mark answered truthfully.

Angela gave Mark a searching look, but before she could speak, Robert Del'arte came up beside his wife.

"Hello, Mark." He turned to his wife. "Angela, I think we should take our seats now. I've saved us two in the middle."

"Yes, Robert, I'm right behind you." Angela leaned close to whisper to Mark. "If you need anything, you'll tell me, won't you, Mark?"

The warm kindness in Angela's face threatened Mark's resolve to handle things alone until his father's return. As the days since his father's departure had stretched to weeks, Mark decided that, if he had to tell anyone, it would be Angela. He opened his mouth to speak.

"Everyone please take your seats. Let's get started." Mayor Umworth rapped his gavel on the podium.

The spell broke. Mark looked toward the Mayor, and then at Angela.

"You'd better go, Angela. I'll tell Mom you asked for her."

Angela started to say something, but stopped. She touched his arm and whispered, "I hope to see you and your parents tomorrow night at the ball, Mark. Please come by if you need anything before then." She turned to join her husband.

Mark watched her move away, torn between relief and disappointment.

An hour later, Mayor Umworth had managed to silence the last shouting match between villagers. Some of the children were watching with huge eyes. They'd never seen their parents and neighbors quarrel in such anger, but once the adults had settled down, the children collected in corners to play, talk or read. Mark lingered in the group around a game of marbles. He'd chosen the spot because he could blend in with his friends, while he listened in on the meeting.

He reached into his coat pocket for the fat chocolate turtle he'd been saving since October. He'd been to village meetings before, and knew that a good sweet made them go much better. But the turtle wasn't in his right pocket, and, after a careful survey of all the others, he realized he'd left the treat at home on the kitchen table.

So far people were still describing the damage done by the marauders, and no one had mentioned a cat. Mark decided to go home, check on his mom and grab the chocolate. He left the meeting and walked toward the cottage, concentrating on his whistling, and trying hard to hit the very highest notes of a difficult melody. At home, he found his mother sleeping peacefully and the missing turtle right where he'd left it.

He was making his way back toward the town hall, when he saw Nathan slogging toward him through the snow. Nathan trailed a fog of cold breath and his head was bowed with bull-like determination to make it up the hill. Marked walked to meet the younger boy.

"Hi, Nathan, what are you doing out here?"

"How'd he do it?" Nathan wheezed. "They breathe like real animals!" The younger boy bounced up and down in goggle-eyed excitement.

"What are you talking about?" Mark asked.

"You must have seen them!"

Mark raised a puzzled eyebrow, a silent request for more information.

"In Father Christmas's window. The cats!" Nathan blurted in frustration. Mark shook his head still looking blank. Then Nathan's words sunk in. The next instant, both boys were racing toward the magic shop.

"Aren't they great?" Nathan whispered, his eyes huge, watching the three sleeping cats. Mark smiled. If Nathan felt this excited about mechanical cats, he would go nuts when he found out these cats were real.

"Yes, they are," Mark whispered back. But his admiration had nothing to do with Mr. Del'arte's talent for illusion. He wasn't crazy, and he hadn't been asleep. He'd seen a real cat at the bakery.

Mark looked closely at each animal. He watched the gray

cat's whiskers twitch in dreamy chase, and he saw the beautiful cat sigh in her sleep. But he knew for certain that the blue-furred cat had been the one at the top of the slide. His fur was really something. Mark's smile broadened—then faded as he took a closer look. The blue's whiskers were singed.

Mark did a slow pan from the cats to the rest of the shop window. His heart sank. In his first excitement, he hadn't noticed the burned paper trees at the edge of the scene.

It looked like the cats were the ones wrecking Christmas.

But he didn't want to believe it. He'd never heard of a cat eating pies and cookies or stealing things. And why would they go anywhere near fire…that didn't make any sense at all.

But if he thought the cats were the culprits, every one else would too.

He decided he'd tell Angela and Robert first, before word got out. If the damage wasn't too bad, maybe they wouldn't be mad at the cats.

Still staring at the animals, Mark said, "Nathan, let's head back to the meeting, and I'll talk to—" Mark looked down expecting to find Nathan beside him, but no Nathan. Mark pivoted in a full circle. "Nathan?" Looking up the lane, Mark saw Nathan tug open one of the heavy doors to the town hall, and disappear inside.

Mark raced back to the meeting, but some of the children were already moving toward their parents. A quiet wave of tugged sleeves and bent ears rippled through the assembly. Mark groaned. Nathan hadn't wasted any time.

Mark could see Angela and Robert Del'arte in the middle of the third row, but he knew he'd never get their attention without attracting every eye in the building. Ten minutes later, the Mayor called for a short break, and Mark wove his way toward the illusionist. But he was not the only one.

"Robert," Nathan's grandmother said in a muted voice, "Nathan just told me about the stuffed cats in your window. He's so excited. If you'll save one for us, it'll be a wonderful Christmas gift for him."

"I'm afraid I have no"…began Mr. Del'arte, leaning down to speak directly to Nathan, but he was interrupted by the arrival of his wife Angela, pulled along by a four-year old girl in a thick, pink sweater.

"Robert, Lisa says she loves cats, and I understand you've put a collection of life-size cats in our window? When did you…?"

"I didn't," answered her husband.

Nathan's brow furrowed in concentration, as a boy who had been standing nearby pulled his father into the circle. "Nathan just saw them," the boy said in a rush, "and he says they look really real, with tails and ears that twitch. And one of them has blue fur! I'd really, really like one. Please, Father?"

"Nathan, you know you're not to leave the building without permission," Nathan's grandmother said, taking him aside.

But throughout the break, a steady stream of parents and children requested cats, and Mr. Del'arte continued to quietly deny placing "a cat of any kind" in his window. When his own sister came over to request a cat for his nephew, he could contain himself no more.

"Of course I would save one for Andrew, but I CAN'T!" he said too loudly. At his sister's look of hurt and disappointment, he explained. "I have only one cat in my entire shop, and it is a tiny pink one that the Duchess ordered months ago for her youngest child. I am pleased to say that I have at last managed to make it purr in a convincing manner. Now that was an extremely interesting challenge, and, even if I do say so myself, I've solved it brilliantly by—"

"Robert," Angela interrupted in a firm tone, "I don't think the Duchess's cat is the one our friends are interested in right now." Her husband looked at the intent faces around him, and took a deep breath.

"I'm sorry to tell you all that I've made only the one pink cat that is neither blue nor twitches. And I can't possibly make enough of those to fill all the requests I've had tonight."

Mark had at last made his way into the circle around the Del'artes. He spoke quietly to Angela, who in turn whispered into her husband's ear. Robert Del'arte nodded once, and then spoke aloud.

"Of course, I appreciate your interest, but if you'll excuse me, I promise to discuss this with all of you later. Right now I need to have a word with Mark."

Mr. Del'arte, Mark, and Angela had just begun talking together when the Mayor called the meeting back to order. Hil, the postmistress, stood up. She had been waiting patiently for her turn to speak, and she began in a clear, commanding voice. "I've been thinking it over, and I just don't believe that our rash of missing food and damaged goods is so mysterious. And I don't think it's any of the children making mischief. I think the problem is—"

"The cats!" Nathan cried out in a piercing voice. He knew what he'd seen, and if Mr. Del'arte hadn't made them, then the cats were real.

"Oh no," groaned Mark.

"Cats? Who said anything about cats?" Mayor Umworth asked rapping his gavel on the podium.

For a moment, no one spoke, and then everyone in the room started talking at once.

"Of course. I knew it all along…"

"Cats can be such troublemakers, they're too independent and stuck up."

"They're just like rodents. Who knows what diseases they've brought with them. To think they were in my house, eating my Christmas pies.

"I'm not so sure cats are to blame," Eva began, but at that moment, Nathan tapped at the Mayor's elbow.

"Whaaa…? Oh, yes, Nathan. What is it child? I'm a bit busy at the moment."

Nathan beckoned the mayor down to five-year-old height, and whispered in his ear. "Really? Are you certain? Wellllll…" was all the villagers heard, even though every person in the room leaned toward the podium, like a field of cornstalks in a stiff breeze. The Mayor stood upright and addressed the assembly.

"It seems Nathan has discovered the hideout of the culprits responsible for the recent havoc in our homes and shops. I suggest we reconvene in front of the Del'arte's. Furthermore, to maintain the advantage of surprise, I suggest we proceed there as quietly as possible."

Pausing only long enough to don coats, hats and gloves, most of the population of Dreamhaven stepped out of the hall and down the main street. Some villagers were angry and ready to punish the cats severely. Others weren't so sure a five-year-old should be allowed to disrupt a town meeting. Many were curious to see if one of the cats really was blue.

But everyone wanted to get to the bottom of the thefts and destruction so they could focus on celebrating Christmas.

CHAPTER FORTY-NINE

Friends or Foes

$\mathcal{D}$reamhaven stood bright beneath a round moon as the villagers formed a hushed circle facing the window of the magic shop. Despite the tension in the air, a whisper of surprised delight rippled round the circle: The sleeping cats looked appealing, innocent, and nothing like determined thieves and vandals.

"Oh, look, look at the cats."

"Is that really blue fur?"

Nick slept tucked beside the miniature miller's wheel. Smoke lay on his back, softly snoring on the bank of the make-believe river. And Rose nestled beside Smoke in the exact spot the villagers would be standing if they were small enough to be in Father Christmas's window scene.

"Are they real, Mama?" an excited child asked in a loud voice.

All three cats startled awake, rising to their feet in fluid motion. They looked out the window at the people looking in at them.

Smoke spoke in a low voice, "We don't want to act guilty and ruin any chance to live here. Everything could be fine—"

"But we should have a plan," Nick cut in.

Rose knew what the plan was. "If anything happens, split up and run for the beacon. Meet there as soon as you can."

"I think we should—" Nick began.

"Trust me, Nick." Rose said.

At the tone of her voice, Nick closed his mouth and nodded his agreement.

A key turned in the lock, and a tall man stepped into the shop. He took a quick, appraising look at the damage, and then, with knotted brows moved toward the cats. They tensed, but did not run. Instead, they walked past him, and led the way into the snow-covered street.

They met the people of Dreamhaven in wary silence, watching the villagers for any movement in their direction. Bart's treachery remained a raw wound. They might face hard decisions once they reached the beacon, but eluding capture was an easy and unanimous choice now.

Mark watched the blue cat from the moment he stepped into the street, and when their eyes met, Mark couldn't help himself. He smiled.

"There are signs of a fire in my shop—and I think these cats started it," said Mr. Del'arte.

Some of the villagers gasped, but many only nodded with pursed lips. Mark's stomach tightened. Shift's talk of old fears and people choosing easy scapegoats rang in his ears. He could see that the cats felt the swing of human emotions like a surging tide. The hackles on all three rose and they came to their feet.

"Oh, no, Robert, I hope you're wrong," said Angela.

"But who else could have done it, my dear? And look, this one has singed whiskers. That puts him very close to the fire, if not marking him as the one who started it."

"A word please, Robert," said Mayor Umworth. He beckoned the illusionist away from the cats.

As the villagers talked among themselves, Mark looked into the blue cat's eyes. The animal was a scrapper and had obviously seen hard times, but Mark sensed no meanness in him, and things still didn't make sense. But everyone wanted an easy answer. And it would be even better if the culprits were outsiders. That way no one in the village was to blame.

"With all three of them gone bad, there's only one solution," said a man behind Mark.

Mark's throat went raw with dread. He knew that Shift would want him—would expect him—to trust his instincts and do something to help the cats. Mark wanted to be that brave.

He just didn't know how in real life.

He wanted to scoop the cats into his arms and protect them. But he'd never be able to hold all three, and he suspected that any sudden move would put action in motion that would doom the cats instantly.

So instead of approaching them and scaring them now, he wrapped his arms around his own shivering body. He needed to concentrate. If the cats were found guilty, he could at least make a screaming run at them. With luck they'd scatter, and get away. He didn't know how they'd survive the winter, and he'd probably never see them again.

But at least he'd buy them a last chance.

Heroes

Nick sensed rising anger in the villagers, and he started to signal Rose and Smoke to run for it. But before he could, Smoke nudged his sister, and together they edged out of the circle of light. Nick felt sad that they'd split up this way, and he'd likely never see his friends again. But if he stayed put, it would give them more time to get away—maybe back into the cold and snow, but away from the angry humans.

Nick was disappointed in the villagers. Despite the weasels, and his tiff with Smoke, Nick had had a good feeling about this place. For one thing, he'd been sleeping nightmare-free. He still hadn't reached his other eight lives, but sound sleep was a huge improvement.

And the boy…when the young human called out to him with such happiness, Nick had been surprised, and downright shocked at how much he wanted to respond. Now, they stood only two feet apart. But the smell of hot fear rolled off the boy's body, ratcheting Nick's anxiety even higher.

Mayor Umworth and Robert Del'arte stepped apart, ending their low conversation. Angela Del'arte touched her husband's arm and began whispering to him fiercely as the Mayor turned to the villagers.

"I think it best if all the children are returned to their homes and tucked into bed—immediately," said the Mayor in a loud announcement. "After all, they need to rest if they're going to dig into the Fabulous Frozen Fantasma tomorrow night." He smiled with false joviality. "Cole, Worter, a word please."

As the two men joined the Mayor, Mark moved closer, straining to hear their conversation.

"Wait until all the children are gone before you round them up," the Mayor ordered.

Mark turned away feeling sick. The time had come to do his best for the cats. The last time he saw them they'd be fleeing from him in terror, but better that then doing nothing. Mark braced for his move. But, as if his body belonged to someone else, he stepped into the center of the circle, placing himself between the villagers and Nick.

"Please—" Mark rasped. He cleared his throat and spoke again, louder. "Please. I'd like to say something." He could hear how weak his voice sounded. But he was all the cats had.

The villagers turned to face Mark in shocked silence. He looked into the faces of the Mayor, his teacher, his neighbors and his friends. They were staring at him, brows knitted, waiting. Mark could feel his knees shaking. He wished his mother were here to help him. He took a deep breath. "We don't know for sure that these cats are the troublemakers. Cats don't steal things. And have you ever seen a cat eat apple pie? Why would they play with flaming candles?"

For a moment, no one spoke. Then Mr. Worter spoke up.

"Mark, if it wasn't them, then who's doing all the nasty things in town?" He asked. "My whole larder's been raided. I've got to accept food from friends for my family's Christmas meal."

Mark's mind stalled despite his racing heart. That was the problem, if not the cats, then who? "I don't know," he finally answered between stiff lips.

The people Mark had known all his life stood around him, no longer willing to look him in the eye. What had he expected? Even his own father didn't listen to him. Mark's face went red with shame, and he slumped, exhausted. He had nothing left to lose. But the cats did.

"Even if they are guilty, do they deserve to die?" he asked aloud, looking first at Mr. Worter and then around the circle of villagers. "What if they're just doing their best to survive?" No one spoke, and the children broke into tears.

"Look, look at the cats!" Angela Del'arte said from behind Mark. "Look what they've got."

Smoke and Rose appeared from around the corner of the shop. Each dragged the body of a dead weasel.

A wave of relief swept through Mark. Weasels! He'd known it. He'd known the cats weren't to blame.

But he still had to convince the rest of the villagers to let them live. "Instead of condemning these cats, maybe we should call them heroes," Mark said in a firm voice, pointing to each of the cats in turn. "Their wounds and burnt fur are battle scars from fighting the real culprits—the weasels," Mark continued, pointing to the dead animals at the cats' feet. "Think about it. We've all seen what a mess weasels can make if they put their minds to it. And the weasels have stolen from the village for years. They've just been smarter about hiding their tracks this time."

"That's exactly what I've been trying to say," said Postmistress Hil. The weasels have a history of stealing from us."

A murmur of agreement moved through the villagers.

Mark turned to Robert Del'arte. "I believe these cats risked their lives to save your home and shop, Mr. Del'arte." he said.

Angela nodded agreement. Her husband paused to consider. Then he looked from his wife to Mark.

"Maybe you're right, Mark," he replied.

"I knew they were good cats," announced Nathan.

"But how did they get here?" asked Hil.

"Obviously, someone abandoned them," a man said.

Eye-Witness

Mark turned toward the familiar voice. Over the heads of the villagers, he locked eyes with his father. Mark felt like he'd been hit by lightning. All his blood seemed to rush to his face, and his whole body trembled. His hands clenched into tight fists, but he couldn't seem to make the rest of his body move at all. It was just as well. He didn't know if he wanted to run to his father—or bolt in the opposite direction.

His father's eyes went bright with unshed tears. His head nodded just a fraction, as if he'd felt Mark's emotions in his own body. Sean looked down at the snow beneath his boots, and brushed a gloved hand over his face in one rapid movement. When his head came up, he no longer looked at Mark. Instead he addressed his friends and neighbors who were waiting for him to continue.

"Whoever abandoned these cats was a fool," Sean said in a rough voice. "Mark's right. They're brave animals. I arrived just as a weasel tipped the flaming star candle and ran for its life. I tried the door, but it was locked. I was going to break in, but the cats were already in motion. The blue one tore off the flaming paper, and I saw them knock over a vase of water onto the flames. They…" When Sean had finished telling what he'd seen, he turned to face his son, looking him right in the eye. "Mark's right. We should be thanking these cats," he said.

Mark couldn't speak. Finally, he nodded once.

At that moment, Joycelyn and David arrived with Eva and a tall man wearing a shiny top hat over his flowing gray hair. Joycelyn held Stephan in her arms. "Sorry we're late to the meeting," she apologized, nodding to the assembled neighbors. "But Eva came to get us and—why is everyone out in the street?" She finished.

Stephan caught sight of Rose and wriggled, laughing aloud, trying his best to reach her.

"I'll be right back," Rose said to Smoke and Nick. I see a friend of mine." She ran to David, who bent down to lift Rose to Stephan. The child laughed with delight as the dreamdancer licked his baby face. Smoke and Nick grinned. It was the happiest they'd seen Rose since the day Adele had stepped through the garden gate and left.

"Well, Stephan may not know exactly what a cat is, but he knows he wants one," laughed Joycelyn. "Are they looking for homes?"

Rose purred in the musician's arms.

"Yes!" Said Mark. He turned to Nick. "If he's willing, the one with the blue fur and singed whiskers is mine," he added in a gentle voice.

Nick rose to his feet at the invitation in the human's voice and eyes. He felt as if he had a sudden, undeniable hunger to be with the boy. He started forward, but then stopped. Nick looked back in time to see Smoke shift his face from sorrow to brave encouragement.

Nick turned and retraced his steps. Brushing hard against Smoke, he sat down at his friend's side. Nick steeled himself. He wouldn't look into the boy's eyes again.

Mark felt certain he knew what had just happened. He and Shift had faced so many challenges side-by-side…

"And two cats would be even better," the boy's voice rang out. He dropped to his knees and opened his arms.

Nick and Smoke both stared at Mark, and then at each other. As one they turned to Rose, cuddled in David's arms. She grinned her happiness and nodded. Nick and Smoke raced to Mark. He lifted the friends in his arms and buried his face in their fur.

M. Marveilleux, the man in the top hat, gestured toward Smoke and leaned down to whisper in Eva's ear. "Eva, eez the grey one not zee perfect model for the sculpture we discussed earlier today?"

"Oh, yes, Henri. He's perfect," she answered in a whisper to match her friend's.

M. Marveilleux raised his voice, addressing himself to Mark. "Eef you would permit me, Mark, I would like to borrow theez one, for several hours tomorrow," he said, pointing to Smoke. "He eez a magnificent example of felis catus domesticus." The famous artist straightened, clicked his heels together, and, sweeping the top hat from his head, he bent in a splendid bow to Smoke.

Smoke's instant purr seemed almost as big as his new name.

"I think that can be arranged, M. Marveilleux," Mark laughed.

CHAPTER FIFTY-TWO

Father and Son

Later that night, Mark and Sean sat in silence over the remains of a cold meal of meat and cheese. Minette slept in the bedroom, unaware that her husband had returned. Mark was in no hurry to tell her.

The cats lay grooming in Sean's overstuffed chair by the hearth, where the fire had burned down to embers in the grate. Neither Sean nor Mark moved to rebuild the flame. Mark stared at the table, but saw nothing.

"Mark, I don't know how to start…" Sean's voice trailed off.

The brass pendulum of the wooden clock swung back and

forth, marking minutes of thick silence.

"Why did you leave?" Mark asked, still not looking at his father, his voice tight. Sean leaned across the wooden table toward Mark.

"I really did set out to find your mother a dog. I thought it might help her somehow…make her happier. But once I got to Dellnor, I just kept going. It was as if something inside me had to keep moving—"

Mark got up to stand in front of the fire, his back to his father.

"I don't blame you for being angry, Mark. I wish I could explain what happened, but—" His father took a deep breath and started again. "I know I've no excuse. Since your mother got worse last month, I've been lost. And once I left Dreamhaven, it was as if I became someone else, someone I didn't even recognize. A man I'd be ashamed to know," he added in a lower voice.

Mark did not respond.

"I never, ever meant to run from you or your mom. Please believe me. It was the pain of losing her I was trying to outrun… and my own cowardice. I didn't know if I could watch her slip away. I love her so much—" Sean's voice cracked. He brought both hands to his face.

Mark turned around to look at his father, but did not move to comfort him.

When Sean regained some control, he looked into Mark's eyes and sat up straighter. "I can't say how sorry I am that I've hurt you. I know I've let you down. I love you, Mark. More than I've ever been able to tell you. It's just that your dreams—"

Mark twisted away, and stalked toward the stairs to his loft.

"I've been so afraid your dreams would take you away too— one way or another."

Mark stopped. He dropped his head remembering what Shift had said about his father's fears. Slowly, he turned to look into his father's face. A wave of weariness washed over him that made his bones too heavy to hold up. The next thing he knew, he was sitting on the bottom stair, facing his father.

Sean rose from the table to kneel at his son's feet. "Tonight, when I watched you defending those animals, I saw a good man standing there. I felt proud. You stood up for what you believed in." His voice dropped to a whisper. "You stood by your mother, when I couldn't. I know now that your dreams have taught you things I can't—and your courage isn't just a fantasy. You're the real hero of Dreamhaven, Mark."

Mark stared at his father, lips parted in shock, until Sean looked away.

A long time later, Mark put his hand on his father's shoulder. Sean let out a ragged breath.

"I hope someday I'll earn your forgiveness, son."

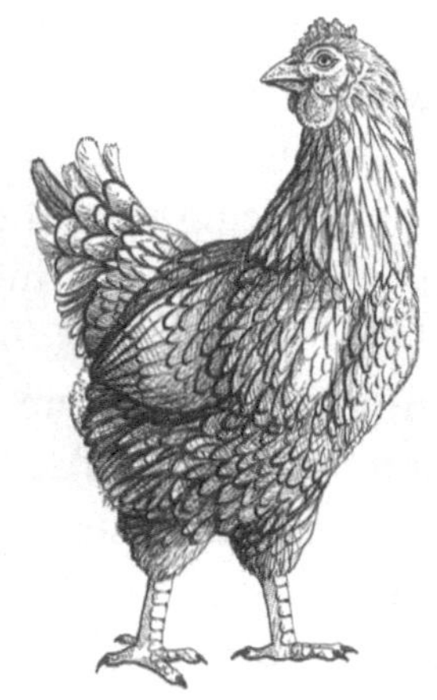

CHAPTER FIFTY-THREE

Boogle Christmas Eve

The district mailman yawned as he arrived home in his faraway village. The previous night had been cold, but storm free, and he'd made very good time.

"Let's get you fixed up with some fresh hay and a warm blanket, Matilda," he whispered to his horse. "It's the least I can do to thank you for getting me home in time to celebrate Christmas with my family."

The weasels awoke in the back of the mail cart.

"Hey, we've stopped."

"Where are we?"

"Let's find out."

Leaping from the cart, they ran until they slipped through the spaces in a nearby fence. Darting over the snow, around rotting rubbish and empty ale kegs, they dashed beneath the floor of the green-shuttered cottage.

"Perfect! There's an easy entrance into the laundry room," the first scout called. The weasels hopped through the hole and followed their noses straight to the kitchen. They gnawed happily on the chicken bones and lumps of molding cheese on the cutting board.

"Looks like we've found a new den," Ralph, the new leader announced as he played with a small gold wedding ring he'd found on the kitchen table. When the boogle finally abandoned the kitchen to explore the three remaining rooms of the messy cottage, they discovered the snoring man in the parlor. He slouched in a grease-stained chair, head thrown back, picket teeth pointed to the ceiling.

"Well, he stinks, but he certainly looks manageable," said Ralph. "And not a cat in sight. Let's get comfortable!"

The boogle got to work, ripping the soft stuffing from Bart's favorite chair.

Christmas Eve, Dreamhaven

The clear sky was a velvet backdrop to countless stars, as villagers and visitors climbed the eastern hill to Clavier's Beacon. At Mark's solemn invitation, Nick, Rose and Smoke leapt to the foot of Clavier's statue. Mark went to stand between his mother and father as each person lit the candle they held. As one, the people saluted Clavier and the three feline Guardians of Dreamhaven.

Nick heard an echo from another night, when he'd stood high atop the Tower of London: "But he will never be Our guardian."

The stupid ol' Ravens had been right. He wished he'd understood. He wished his father could see him now...

A song unlike any other rang out. All eyes turned to the heavens. Hundreds of luminous dreams appeared in the sky above Dreamhaven. The dreams took every imaginable form—and some that have not yet been imagined. Exultant song filled the night, and the people and animals of Earth lifted their voices in answer.

Rose heard Clavier's unforgettable voice inside her.

"Well done, Rose. In thanks for the courage and love you, Smoke and Nick have brought to Dreamhaven, we offer you each one wish come true."

"We passed the test," Rose purred to Smoke and Nick.

"What test?" they asked in unison.

"You'll have to trust me," Rose grinned. "Make a wish."

Without a word, Smoke closed his eyes and dipped his chin in concentration. Nick and Rose exchanged a happy grin over Smoke's head, and then Rose closed her eyes.

Nick had always wanted just one thing: to live his nine lives like every other cat.

He looked at his friends, Smoke and Rose, sitting tall, eyes closed, heads bowed. Then he looked at his human. Mark smiled back at him.

"Maybe one life with good friends is enough," he thought. Nick closed his eyes before he could change his mind. "Please grant my friends whatever will make them happiest."

The song ended, the last notes echoing over the mountaintops. The dreams that belonged in Dreamhaven lingered, waiting for their owners to sleep and claim them.

One-by-one the other dreams became shooting stars. They streaked through the sky in a dazzling farewell, as they spread across the Earth to unite with their dreamers.

The villagers stood in silence, looking up into the sky until the last dream disappeared from sight. Each villager, young and old touched the hem of Clavier's bronze skirt in thanks. Then they and their new guardians descended to the Town Hall.

Fabulous

When everyone had gathered inside the Town Hall, the Duchess pulled on a green velvet ribbon. A red silk curtain rose in the air, and the Fabulous Frozen Fantasma shimmered in luscious splendor.

M. Marveilleux had earned the shiny new medal pinned to his chest. He'd worked non-stop to finish in time. And his masterpiece stood flawless. Rose and Nick looked up at the glory of ice cream, and then both turned surprised eyes to Smoke.

As it turned out, Eva had dreamt the Christmas Vision, and Smoke had kept her secret to himself. The Fabulous Frozen Fantasma had been carved into a twelve-foot tall feline in a jacket with cat's-eye buttons. The handsome cat held an ice-cream cloud in his paws.

"Oh, yes, yes indeed," Eva assured everyone. "It's a perfect likeness to the cats in my dream."

That's when M. Marveilleux clicked his heels, gave Eva one of his fancy bends and asked her to dance. And boy, could she dance. The villagers clapped as the pair whirled to the music.

The only one at all peevish was the Duchess. "I think it's highly unusual, and very likely illegal for a living, breathing cat to pose for a dream sculpture," she pointed out, poised beside the towering dessert. But as her first oversized spoonful of Fabulous Frozen Fantasma melted on her tongue, she seemed to forgive and forget. She took a large helping for herself. Then she ate another for every member of her retinue, including the Duke, their four children, the valet, all eleven ladies in waiting, the nine coachmen and Fifi.

"Fifi, another bowl please. I'm certain this 'Duchess Delight' is the richest, most delicious flavor anyone has ever tasted," she exclaimed in a loud voice.

But in ice cream appreciation, the Duchess had nothing on Nick. "Didn't I tell you?" he said to Rose and Smoke between licks. "Isn't ice cream something?"

By the time the three cats waddled out of Town Hall, Nick felt ready to sleep right through Christmas morning. They'd already been given the gift of loving homes, and it had been a long, nap-deprived road from Bart's to Dreamhaven. Smoke and Nick wished Rose a Merry Christmas and then jumped to Mark's shoulders for the ride home.

But when the family got to their cottage, they discovered Father Christmas had left one more gift. In a basket beside the hearth, lay a blue-eyed pup. His thick fur was gray and white, and one look into his huge eyes convinced everyone that he was gentle and smart. No one moved until Mark crossed the room, petted the dog, and reached for the card. When he looked up he was smiling and his cheeks were wet.

"To Minette, from Father Christmas," he read aloud.

Minette looked from her son to her husband in surprise. Then her smile lit the whole room. She knelt, reached into the basket and took the dog in her arms. "Zeb," she said. "We'll call him Zeb."

Nick and Smoke wasted no time. They launched right into Zeb's first lesson: "Our bowl, your bowl." As Zeb resettled into his basket, the cats climbed the stairs to Mark's loft. After a few licks of mandatory grooming, Nick and Smoke snuggled in beside the boy. All three closed their eyes.

For the first time since arriving in Dreamhaven, Nick floated helpless in his familiar nightmare. His nine stars sparkled against the black. And Nick's heart sank. He'd almost accepted his fate—just one life. But in Dreamhaven, at least he hadn't faced this. He closed his eyes. He'd had a lifetime of gut-wrenching horror. He already knew what happened next.

"Please tell me you're not gonna sleep all night," said Smoke. "That would be such a waste of good lives."

Nick opened his eyes. Mark and Smoke stood beside the pine tree. But the pine tree was purple and instead of snow, the ground was tiger fur. And next to Smoke he saw a—well he wasn't sure what kind of animal had an armored tail and the upper body of an owl, but all three were grinning at him.

"Where am I? Did I—? Is this—?" Nick spluttered.

"Yes you did, and it is," said Smoke. "Welcome to the first of your other nine lives." Smoke clicked his hind paws together and bent forward in a dramatic bow. Mark applauded and Shift grinned at Smoke's perfect imitation of M. Marveilleux.

Nick turned in a slow circle. To his right, he saw a sleek ship with blue sails anchored in a glittering red sea. Behind him, a dozen metal boxes with yellow bird legs ran through a cabbage field. One of the boxes jumped into the air and a piece of bread popped out the top. To his left, two moons hung in a violet sky. Nick came full circle back to the three smiling faces. He looked at Smoke, afraid to ask.

"But if I've crossed dream into one of my other lives, then you shouldn't be—" Nick broke off.

But Smoke nodded and grinned wider. "I know. I'd run out of lives, and I shouldn't be here. But then there was that part where we each got one wish. I can't say who wished for what. But I can tell you this: You've arrived, I'm here, and Rose is waiting for us aboard that fine ship."

Nick erupted in the loudest purr of his life.

Smoke's was just as loud.

"Come on you two," said Mark, "we've got a whole new world to explore."

Turning to the bright red sea, the four friends fell into step.

About the Author

Tracy Tandy is a freelance writer and the author of *Dreamhaven*; *Alphabet Dreams* with illustrator Lucy Arnold; and *Druk and Mita*, available 2016. Ms. Tandy is never bored, in large part thanks to her opinionated characters, which currently include extraterrestrial detectives and a Bhutanese dragon. She lives with her patient husband and intrepid cat in the San Francisco Bay Area.

www.tracytandy.com